"Am I too close?" Mike asked.

"No. Yes. Let's just say I'm not used to this much, uh, male company."

"So don't think of me as male company. Think of me as a computer tutor."

"That will take some doing," Lori muttered. He hadn't moved any farther away, and it was all she could do to think, period.

"Where was I?" He leaned even closer to her, and she could feel the warmth of him along her back as he studied the screen with her.

His voice rumbled in her ear. "I think it was your interest. I mean, interest in figures. No, I mean the interest figures. On the spreadsheet." He leaned his forehead down to her shoulder. It felt so good to have him there, leaning on her. "Am I making much sense?"

"Not much. But I don't mind...."

Books by Lynn Bulock

Love Inspired

Silhouette Romance

LYNN BULOCK

lives near St. Louis, Missouri, with her husband, two sons, a dog and a cat. She has been telling stories since she could talk and writing them down since fourth grade. She is the author of nine contemporary romance novels.

Looking for Miracles
Lynn Bulock

Love Inspired®

Published by Steeple Hill Books™

STEEPLE HILL BOOKS

Steeple
Hill™

ISBN 0-373-87103-1

LOOKING FOR MIRACLES

I can do all things in Christ who gives me strength.
—*Philippians* 4:13

To Joe, always
and
To CJB, who never ceases to amaze me.

Chapter One

Lori Harper needed a miracle. It didn't have to be a big, showy miracle. Not like the time she and Tyler were down to peanut butter, crackers and half a bag of flour in the whole house and Tyler had reached his hand between the couch cushions and pulled out a twenty-dollar bill like a magician pulling a rabbit out of his hat.

She pushed her shoulder-length blond hair out of her face and shifted her unwieldy body on the edge of the bed. It didn't even have to be a medium-size miracle. There had been plenty of those in her life, and she was thankful for them. Of course there were times when even miracles didn't help, or she wouldn't be in the fix she was in.

She still didn't understand why Gary had to go

and run the car off the road last August or why he
didn't get out before the car sunk in the lake. There
had been no miracles that day, unless it was the
kind crew from the county fire-and-rescue team that
had broken the horrible news.

The young woman, especially, had been wonderful. Carrie had helped Lori face all the awful
arrangements. She'd even bullied Gary's boss,
Clyde Hughes, into giving them a replacement car,
even though Gary had no insurance, and no pay-
check coming except from the week he died. Carrie
had stood her ground and argued toe-to-toe with
the prominent businessman in a way that Lori
couldn't imagine doing.

That was a minor miracle, even though Gary
hadn't left any others in his wake. He did the best
he could as a father and husband until the day he
died. Lori wished he could have lived long enough
to be here today. Even more, Lori wished she'd told
Carrie about this baby. She hadn't been showing
noticeably in August, and didn't feel like seeming
even more pathetic than she did already in this awful place with only her son Tyler for company.

Lori arched her back. The only thing moving did
was remind her that her swollen belly dwarfed the
rest of her slender body. It didn't ease her discomfort. Still, she considered herself fortunate. Even if
it was out here with no neighbors, at least they had

a roof over their heads, and it was warm and dry and there weren't any crawly things in it, like that one apartment in Kansas City.

A sharp wave of pain across her belly brought Lori back to the present. Yes, this time a little miracle would do just fine. Like the time the lady from the next farm over, where they had a telephone, stopped by the way she did that once before Gary told her to leave them alone. Right now she'd even take Gary's old boss coming out to ask his aggravating, enigmatic questions.

"Anybody," Lori said aloud through dry lips. "Anybody at all would be a miracle." And she needed that miracle soon. Because this time Lori Harper had to admit something to herself. Unlike the time with the peanut butter, when she and Tyler would have been hungry and uncomfortable, she was in real trouble now.

This time it looked as though she was going to give birth in a trailer with no phone, miles from anyone except her five-year-old son. It hadn't been an easy pregnancy, and if she was reading the signs right, she had maybe an hour until the baby arrived. This time, Lori admitted, if she didn't get her miracle she could very well die.

"I hate my job." Mike Martin didn't answer his friend Carrie Collins because he knew she wasn't talking to him. She was talking to Dogg, who took up most of the bench seat of the pickup between them. The big black-and-tan shepherd thumped his tail and moaned softly at the attention from Carrie. "I hate my job, I hate my life, I hate..."

"Aw, knock it off, Carrie," Mike told her. "You don't hate your job. You're one of the best fire-and-rescue officers in the county, maybe even in the state of Missouri. You only hate the fact that it's winter, it's cold and you've got to go out in the middle of nowhere and remind some woman she's a widow."

"Like it's going to surprise her, I'll bet," Carrie said glumly, still holding Dogg's massive tawny head in her hands. "But still, why do I have to do this?"

"Because it's your job," Mike reminded her, looking over at the slim redhead. "And despite saying you hate it, you're very good at it. Besides, you took the original call on this one. And you insisted that Ms. Harper be the one that the department took up their collection for. And let's add the fact that the captain knew that being a woman, you'd give this part of the job the right kind of sympathy." What Mike didn't add was that nobody else wanted to touch the assignment with a ten-foot pole, so naturally it fell to the junior member of the team.

That part was unspoken but agreed. "You gonna help out?" Carrie asked him.

Mike snorted. He might be built like a brick wall, but he was more intelligent than one. "Lady, this is your job. I just drive the truck, remember?"

"Drive the truck, dive for things in the pond, do search and rescue with Mister Big here—the whole nine yards," Carrie said. "You should be doing my job, you know."

Mike felt a column of ice replace his spine. He looked straight ahead to where the wipers scraped snow off the windshield. His dark hair was still damp from his shower, and the cold made him shiver. At least he would say it was the cold, and not the thought of doing Carrie's job. "Never in a million years. You do your job, I'll do mine. I can handle driving, diving and spending most of my time waiting between volunteer calls back at the real-estate office. But regular patrol work? No, ma'am. Not in this lifetime."

"Suit yourself. I still say you'd be good at it. How about being backup anyway out here?" Carrie wheedled. "I mean, since my partner deserted me and everything..."

"Bart didn't desert you. He was listening for the dispatcher."

"Yeah, well, only because he'd rather spend the morning waiting for a call that might not come than do what I'm doing." Carrie wore the ghost of a pout on her snub-nosed face.

"Oh, get real," Mike told her. "Anybody would rather do that than go out to a spot ten miles from anyplace and tell some girl her Christmas is going to come from the fire department because she's the most pathetic case they had all year."

Anybody sane, Mike added silently. He'd long ago counted himself among the other part of the population because he would have given his well-muscled right arm to be able to do what the woman sitting next to him did. But like he told her, it wasn't going to happen in this lifetime. This was the closest he was going to get to her kind of work, with good reason. There was enough trouble in his past to convince Mike he wasn't capable of the kind of strength this took.

"You've got a point," Carrie admitted. "And you still haven't answered my question. Are you going to be my backup here?"

Even in the cold Mike could feel himself break out in a sweat. "I hadn't planned on it. I mean, you've got the training in this. I'm just a guy with a truck, the guy who's dumb enough to drive you out here, remember?"

"All too well," Carrie said. "You won't even put on the red suit. Could we at least try the antlers on Dogg?"

"If you want to try antlers on Dogg, go ahead. I am not helping, unless he bites you. Can't let the old EMT training go to waste," Mike said, wondering why he'd even agreed to get out of the truck.

His part of this job had been done in August. He'd taken a johnboat across that pond to where Dogg unmistakably told them there was a body somewhere under the surface. He'd put on his wet suit and probed the murky water until they'd found the battered car that yielded Gary Harper's body still behind the wheel. Facing his widow, even this many months later, was beyond him.

Granted, she might not be that brokenhearted to be a widow. Everybody in the department pegged Gary Harper for a small-time drug runner, out on parole this time for less than a year. The car had yielded evidence that he'd moved here to Franklin County to set up his old trade of running a meth lab. He probably hadn't been any prize to live with.

A battered mailbox alerted Mike that the turnoff to the trailer was ahead. "Hold on to your hat. Things are about to get bumpier."

"Like that's possible." Their heads nearly hit the ceiling of the big truck. Even Dogg gave a deep "woof" of discomfort when they settled back into the ruts of the nearly nonexistent lane to the house.

They jounced down the ruts for almost a half mile. At the end of the ruts was a single-wide mobile home in poor condition. There were lights on behind two of the windows. At least that was encouraging.

Looking at the mobile home, anger rose in Mike. He wondered how anybody, even a thug like Gary Harper, could let his family live out here. Couldn't he have provided something better when he was alive? The aluminum siding of the trailer was gray and dented. Two cracked concrete blocks served as the only stoop at the front door. The whole place had such an air of neglect, Mike wondered if anyone would answer the door, even with the lights on.

Carrie got out of the truck cab and coaxed Dogg to stand up. The big German shepherd looked back at Mike with a questioning look. He didn't shake off the fabric antlers, but he seemed to beg Mike to do it for him.

"Sorry, buddy. You let Carrie do that. Now go to the door with her."

The dog leapt down with a resigned air and followed Carrie. Mike shut off the engine and got out to stretch his legs. Carrie went up to the door and knocked.

She stood, head cocked, for a long time. "There's somebody in there. I can hear them," she said, turning her head toward Mike.

"Kids?" Mike asked her. He hadn't thought of

that possibility. He breathed a silent prayer. *Please, no kids. I can handle anything else, but no kids.*

Carrie knocked again. "Franklin County Fire and Rescue. Please open the door," she called loudly. Now things were getting serious.

"I can hear bumping and scraping inside. I wonder if…"

Before she had time to say anything else, the door swung slightly open. From where Mike stood, he could tell that it was blocked from opening all the way. Carrie looked back at him, her pale complexion paling even more. "C'mon, Mike. I need backup here."

He was at the door in an instant, heart racing. Mike was hoping for some beefy accomplice of Harper's, a big guy he could take out by brute strength. No such luck. Instead, a small boy with wispy blond hair stood in the doorway. He looked to be maybe five years old.

The child struggled with the chair that blocked the door. "Had to get it to unlock the chain. I can't reach the chain by myself. But the chair's heavy," he said, panting, as he tried to push the chair away. "I'm Tyler. Are you here about Mama?" he asked, still struggling with the chair.

"Let me," Mike said, picking it up with one hand and getting it out of the path of the door. "Can we come in?"

"Sure." The little boy motioned them in. "Mama says you guys are her miracle. She says the baby's coming. Are we going to get to ride in a police car?" His blue eyes sparkled with anticipation.

Carrie was already pushing her way down the narrow hall from the trailer's main room to the bedrooms. "Something better, Tyler," she said over her shoulder. "How do you like trucks?"

"Cool." The boy grabbed Mike's hand. "Come on and get Mama. She likes trucks, too."

At the touch of the small boy's hand, time telescoped for Mike. He went down on his knees next to him, looking at the boy. He saw so much.

There was more in this moment than a slender child in battered blue jeans and a sweatshirt. For Mike Martin there was a reliving of a very similar scene. In a scary instant he knew what was behind that boy's wide blue eyes. Here the kid was, trying to get help for the most important person in his world, wanting reassurance that everything would be all right.

For this child it probably would be. Mike looked into his eyes. "We'll go take care of your mom. It's going to be okay, Tyler." How he wished with all his heart that somebody had taken time to say those words years ago, when he'd been the boy in blue jeans.

Of course in his case, any such reassurances would have been a lie. Nothing anybody did that cold morning long ago could have made everything all right again in Mike's world. For the child in front of him there was still a chance. So for this child, Mike had to fight his horror, his fear, and deal with the situation. He stood up.

"Take me to your mom. Ms. Collins doesn't know much about babies."

Tyler looked at him in disbelief. "She's a girl, isn't she? I thought they all knew about that stuff."

Mike shook his head. "That girl knows more about cars than babies. I guess that's why I'm here," he told Tyler, only realizing the truth of it as he said it. He'd wondered all morning why he had agreed to drive Carrie out here instead of taking Dogg and going back home the way he should have. Now he knew. Just let me do all right, he said silently.

He looked down at the brave little kid leading him down the hall. It had to be all right, just for him. Mike took a deep breath and pushed through the doorway.

The man Tyler led into the room filled the doorway. Lori felt dwarfed by his presence. He looked calm, though, a lot calmer than Gary would have been in the same situation. "I'm so glad you're here. It really is a miracle."

"Not quite." The red-haired woman in uniform looked at the man and telegraphed something to him silently. "But it looks like what we came for will have to wait."

Lori laughed nervously. "Yes, it does. Do either of you have any training in catching babies?"

"Mike does. He used to be an EMT. I mean, I've had the basics, in theory, but I've never used it. Mike?"

The big man nodded, and crossed the small room. "Sure have. Where are we, Mrs. Harper?"

"Lori." This was no time to be formal. "And I think we're at the point where I hope you're either driving an ambulance or you have a radio, Mike."

The man's smile was rueful. "Can't say I can help you either way. But I do have a cellular phone in the truck. What do you say we call the county emergency guys on duty, who have the real ambulance and radio, and try to meet them on the closest main road? Do you think we have enough time for that?"

"I hope so." Lori struggled to speak while she felt a contraction building. "With Tyler, things were pretty quick, once they started happening, and I expect it will be quick this time, too."

"What does the doctor say?" The man's large

hands were gentle as he helped her off the bed and into a standing position. Lori wished she could avoid his question.

"Nothing. I haven't seen one," Lori admitted. His intake of breath was sharp, and an emotion that could have been fear or anger flashed through his dark eyes. "We moved out here before I knew I was, uh, in the family way, and then Gary had the car all day working in Friedens, and after August I never got around to finding somebody..." She trailed off. How could she tell a stranger that there was no money for a doctor? "Will we all fit in that truck outside? I won't leave Tyler here."

"There's no way we'd leave him," the woman in uniform said. "Not alone, anyway." She looked at the man. "I was thinking maybe you and Mrs. Harper ought to go on, and the rest of us will stay here until somebody else can come out and get us."

The man shook his head. "Won't work. That dog wouldn't take a command to stay at a strange place without me. How long has it been since you've ridden in the back of a pickup?"

When the woman started to splutter, Mike looked at Lori and winked. It was such a conspiratorial gesture that she had to smile through the wave of pain that threatened to fold her double. "There's no other choice, Carrie. You and the dog can sit in the back. Me and Lori and Tyler'll be up front.

What do you bet we can make it to the main road in less time than EMS does from their end?''

Lori stifled a gasp as her protector guided her back through the trailer and helped her down from the front door to the hard ground. ''Gently, Mike. Hit any bumps wrong and you're going to have to use those EMT skills yourself, I'm afraid.''

He looked her in the face, all traces of teasing gone now. His dark eyes sparkled with a light that pierced Lori deeper than the pain of the contractions. ''I'll take care of you. Don't worry.'' And somehow, looking into those eyes, she knew he was telling the truth.

Chapter Two

This was the strangest trip to the hospital Lori had ever witnessed, much less been part of. The red-haired woman in uniform and the huge German shepherd—was he really wearing reindeer antlers?—were in the back of the truck. It was cold in the cab because Mike's car phone handset was out the open back window, so Carrie could talk to the paramedics while Mike navigated the bumpy road.

Mike had apologized for having to put the phone plug in the cigarette lighter for power. "I never remember to charge the battery."

"Lost the charger, probably," she heard Carrie mutter from outside. Lori had to stop breathing so fast. If they hit one more bump, Tyler was going to get to meet his new brother or sister up close and personal. Tyler looked so small sitting next to her on the seat, bouncing up and down even though he was belted in.

"Isn't this cool, Mama?" His eyes shone. From his perspective, it was probably cool. All of Tyler's passions were involved here: uniformed police officers, big dogs, huge trucks and a man who actually paid attention to him. When she nodded to agree with him, a wave of nausea roared over her.

"Bad move, huh?" Mike looked over at her sharply. How could he drive and keep his eyes on the road yet still monitor how she was feeling?

"Bad move." She held her head still. Things felt better that way. "How far are we from—"

"Meeting the ambulance crew? Tell us, Carrie." Mike turned his head toward the open back window.

Carrie spoke into the phone, then leaned toward the open window. "Maybe five minutes. You going to be able to hang on?"

"Sure." Lori gritted her teeth. She wasn't sure, but she was going to have to be, for Tyler's sake, for the baby's sake, even for the sake of the large man driving the truck. He didn't look ready to deliver a baby.

The next five minutes seemed more like five hours. Lori would have burst into tears of relief when the yellow ambulance pulled up to the truck, but she lacked the energy. Mike braked and vaulted out of his side of the truck. "Don't you dare try to get out on your own," he warned. "Hey, Kenny, Rosa, this lady's about to have a baby. How about some real quick movement this way?"

Before Lori could say anything, she was on a stretcher pulled up to the cab of the truck. In moments, she was looking up at the ceiling of the moving ambulance while someone with cold, sure hands was assessing the situation.

"Hi, I'm Rosa." The dark-haired woman smiled. "You've got a head nearly crowning here, but you probably knew that already. Mike said to tell you that they'd follow us there and meet us at the hospital. He said not to worry about Tyler."

"I won't. Right now I've got all I can worry about right here."

It was there in the ambulance, holding Rosa's hand, that Lori had to come to terms with what she'd known for months. Gary was really dead. She was really doing this on her own, and it wasn't getting any easier.

When Lori thought about Gary, she couldn't feel any pain. Just a sense of peace, something telling her that maybe the most troubled soul she'd ever known had finally found rest.

She wondered if he was watching them somehow, could see what was going on. There was no time to wonder. Another contraction engulfed her. The ceiling of the ambulance blurred. When they hit a rut on the road she stifled a yelp. "Go ahead and yell if it will make you feel any better." Rosa was still right there with her. "Anything that will keep you from giving in to that urge to push right now would be welcome."

Lori managed a weak smile. "I guess you would rather the doctors at the hospital delivered this baby."

Rosa nodded. "I've caught a couple myself, but it's always good to have help. It would be more comfortable for you in the long run, too."

"Then I hope the hospital isn't too much farther." That ceiling was starting to blur again. This baby was going to be here soon, wherever they were.

"Am I a big brother yet?" Tyler asked, looking around the commotion of the emergency room.

"We'll find out. It wouldn't surprise me at all." Carrie held his hand and craned her neck over the crowd. "You see anything?"

Mike's vantage point was better, but he still had no indication of where Kenny and Rosa might have taken their precious cargo. "Nothing yet. Let's ask at the desk."

"Yeah, she just made it." The triage nurse came

around the counter and went down to Tyler's height. "You have a very pretty baby sister. Of course she might look all red and squashy to you, but she looks pretty good to Mom right now. If you wait about twenty minutes more, we'll get you back there to see her, once we clean them both up."

Tyler's brow wrinkled. "How'd they get dirty?"

The nurse laughed. "Well, they didn't, exactly. But being born is pretty messy." She looked at Carrie and Mike. "Maybe one of your friends can take you to look at the vending machines while we let your mom know you're here."

"Cool. Do they have candy bars?" Tyler looked around for the machines.

"They sure do. And really good chips." Carrie led him to the small room off the hallway where the machines were. Naturally she'd take the easy part. Mike straightened up.

"Guess that means I'm going back with Mrs. Harper. You say she had a girl?"

The nurse nodded. "At least eight pounds. And she really is pretty. I wasn't lying to her brother. Rough way to start out life, though."

Lori looked beautiful but frail propped up in her hospital bed holding a very new baby. They were an oasis of calm in the emergency room. Only a curtain separated the bay that held mother and child from organized chaos on either side of them. Mike hadn't looked in the other cubicles, but one seemed to be occupied by someone elderly and quite deaf, while the other seemed to hold a brace of wildcats, or maybe just an unhappy toddler and mother.

Lori looked up from the bundle in her arms. "Hi. You made it. Isn't she something?" Her smile was touched with exhaustion. "I'm still figuring out what to call her. Gary was so sure this was going to be a boy. He said it would be Gary, Jr., this time. I can't think of any way to make Gary into a girl's name though."

Mike shook his head. He had no idea what to say to this lady. "Nothing comes to mind right away. Carrie's out getting Tyler a candy bar. The nurses wanted us to hold off bringing him back for a few minutes, give you some more rest time."

Lori smiled again wanly. "Good. I have a feeling rest is going to be in very short supply in a little while. Once they figure out we're both okay, we'll probably go home. With no insurance, they won't keep us long."

"No insurance? Didn't your husband leave you anything? What about Medicaid? Something?"

Lori's eyes clouded. "He hadn't been at his job that long. Gary's boss said we wouldn't be qualified for health insurance until he'd been there for a year anyway and even then not for a baby that was already on the way. Said it was one of those 'preexisting conditions' all the insurance companies talk about.''

Mike suspected that whatever Harper was doing in Friedens, Missouri, it hadn't been the kind of job that came with a medical plan. Meth labs were a little short on benefits. Still, now wasn't the time to bring any of that up. Lori Harper didn't seem to know much about what her husband had really done for a living. There would be plenty of time to break the bad news to her later.

Right now it was time to admire the baby. That was easy to do. She was fairly red and squashy, but she looked a whole lot better than most newborns Mike had seen. At least this one had open eyes of that fuzzy indeterminate blue most newborns sported. And she had hair. Squiffs of blond fuzz poked up all over her head.

She was quiet, too. Mike expected her to be squalling, but the baby was making little noises, most of which sounded fairly content. As if to jinx him once he thought that, her small face screwed up, flushing and ready for a howl. "What's the matter?"

Her mother smiled. "Nothing. She's probably just tired and hungry. So if you don't mind…" She looked at him pointedly. Mike could feel himself turning all kinds of colors once he realized what she was asking.

"I'll be outside here if you need me for anything." It was all he could choke out as he retreated.

The baby's howling stopped almost as soon as he was on the other side of the curtain. Mike fought not to entertain any picture whatsoever of the scene that created the quiet. As he struggled with his thoughts he saw two young men dressed in scrubs rolling a gurney off the elevator and into the E.R.

They rolled it up to the nurses' station, which was empty. Looking around, one of them spotted a very young woman rushing by. "We're here to transfer Harper up to the maternity floor."

He wasn't very quiet, and his partner was even louder. "Yeah, I heard this one was related to that drug dealer we had in August. The one that took the methedrine plunge..."

The young nurse's aide, or whatever she was, finally got the jerk quieted down. Mike steeled himself for what he would find behind the curtain. Maybe they'd been granted a little miracle and Lori would be so wound up in her beautiful new daughter that she hadn't heard what went on.

He couldn't imagine that was true. "Mike?" Her voice was choked and faint.

The baby was still nursing under a white cotton

blanket. Lori's shaking arms could barely hold her. "I wasn't supposed to hear that, was I?"

"Hear what?" He could try to brazen it out for a little while.

"That bit about another Harper. A drug dealer. Again? But he told me he was going straight this time. That he was doing a real job for honest money." Her lips tightened into a thin, white line. Her eyes were huge. "Is that why his boss was so strange? And there was nobody at the funeral?"

Mike came over to her side. He couldn't watch her tremble alone anymore. He put one arm around her shaking one, supporting the baby. "I didn't want to be the one to have to tell you."

"Even out at the trailer, I could tell that. You and Carrie knew something you weren't saying in front of Tyler. Does everybody else in Friedens know this for a fact?"

Mike told her softly, and as gently as possible, what he knew. "Talk around the department was that he was dealing. Maybe even manufacturing."

Lori's expression hardened. "So that drug-informant part of what he told me about being relocated… It wasn't true, was it?"

"It might have been." Mike didn't want to lie to her, but keeping hope in a dead man didn't feel much like a lie. The baby made a little sighing, gulping noise. "Do you want help shifting her around?"

"No, I can manage. I think you can let go now." Lori looked down at his arm, stretched the length of hers. Mike was aware of how soft she was, how fine boned. Her elbow fit in his cupped hand with so much room left over. He let go and looked away.

"I'm sorry."

"Sorry that he died, or sorry you had to be the one to tell me the truth about him?" Lori's voice was sharp. Mike looked back into her face. "That wasn't real nice, I know. But I also know that Gary wasn't a real model citizen in the county. We didn't exactly have a welcoming committee beating a path to our door when we moved in."

"Yeah, well, I'm still sorry he's gone. No matter what he did for a living. I mean, he was probably a good daddy, and now—"

"Don't go there." Lori's voice was still sharp. "If I'm truthful with myself, he was an awful father. He never knew what to do with Tyler, and a new baby wouldn't have made any difference. Finding out about her was probably what made him turn to the drug thing again. It seemed to be the only way he knew how to make money."

Lori's tough facade couldn't last. Mike told himself that, and as he did, he watched her crumble. Her arms beneath the baby shook, and her eyes filled with tears. "Oh, Lord, what am I going to do?"

Suddenly everything caught up with her and she lost what little color she had as silent tears coursed down her cheeks. Mike had no idea what to do besides sit there and pat her arm. He hoped that was okay, because it was the only thing he could do. So for a while they all sat quietly.

The baby nursed. Lori wept. Mike patted her arm. Both of the adults were conscious of the presence of the two young men with the gurney, just beyond the cloth divider. Even this little oasis of calm they had created wouldn't last long. As the last of the calm there trickled away, Mike heard the echoes of Lori's wail in his mind. What *were* they going to do? The thought of leaving this young woman alone to deal with whatever fate handed her was unthinkable.

Now the pittance the department had scraped together for Christmas wasn't enough. For a brave young widow with a five-year-old, it might have been. But not now. Not with this baby, and Lori's new knowledge of her desperate situation. The moment Tyler Harper had opened the door and let Mike into his home, he was hooked. And even for a problem this size, he intended to be part of the solution.

Chapter Three

It took Lori about an hour to get settled in her room on the maternity floor. Brisk nurses whisked her daughter away to be washed, weighed, measured and looked after. Once the baby was out of her arms, Lori sank back into the bed pillows. She was too exhausted and confused to think. Her body ached for a hot shower, but she knew what the nurses would say to that.

She should be making phone calls. But to who? How long would it be until someone told her she had to leave the hospital? "I asked for a miracle," she reminded God out loud. Maybe this looked like a miracle on the other side of heaven, but it sure didn't look like one from under a white cotton blanket in a hospital bed.

Lori let the crisp sheets and firm pillows envelop her. Okay, time to take stock. There *were* miracles here. She'd had the baby in the hospital, surrounded by doctors and nurses, instead of alone in the trailer or in the ambulance on the road. And her daughter was beautiful and healthy, as far as Lori could see.

So the immediate past was full of miracles. As for the near future, Lori wasn't so sure. She felt very fragile just now. Where was her hope right now?

She let out a little laugh. Hope? That was all she could have right now, wasn't it? There certainly wasn't any money around. Or much solid that she could put her hands on. There was a rickety trailer whose rent was paid for maybe two more months. And a rattletrap heap of a car Gary's former employer had been bullied into signing over the title on. Maybe that was her ticket out of this mess, at least for the time being.

Lori dreaded going back to that trailer in the middle of nowhere. It was bad enough when Gary had come home almost every night bringing groceries and bits of the outside world. The last few months had been awful. Now with a new baby, it would be horrible with no other adults, no phone…

A shudder ran through her body. Lori covered her face with her hands, fighting sobs. Was there any hope for the future? As if to answer, a woman walked through the door of the room, pushing a cart. In a plastic bassinet on the cart was the most beautiful baby Lori had ever seen. It was her baby. "Isn't she gorgeous? What's her name?"

"Mikayla Hope." The words popped out before Lori could stop them. The little girl looked pleased with her name somehow. She knew that babies less than a day old didn't smile. But this one seemed to if you looked just right. And nestled back in Lori's arms with the help of the woman, who brought her into the room, she was a warm, welcome weight.

She smelled of mild soap, fresh cotton and some magical scent all her own. "Mikayla Hope," Lori whispered in her ear. The velvet warmth of the baby's face was overpowering. Here was her little miracle.

As if on cue Tyler burst into the room, followed by Carrie. "Hey, there's our baby. And she's not dirty at all," he said, crowding up to the bed. "What's her name, Mama?"

"This is Mikayla Hope. Come up and see her. Gently." Tyler scrambled onto the bed. He reached out one hand and stroked the baby's cheek.

"Hi, Mikayla. I'm Tyler. I'm your big brother." His voice was soft. "She feels good."

"I'll bet she does." Carrie pulled up the bedside chair. "Mikayla Hope, huh? Does a certain some-one know about the Mikayla part?"

"Not yet. I just found out myself." Carrie's look was one of pure confusion, and Lori hastened to explain. "The nurse asked what her name was, and the words just came out. But it's perfect. I can't see her being anybody else, can you?"

Carrie peered over at the swaddled baby. "I don't know. I think she looks like Mr. Peanut in that wrapping. Or I guess Ms. Peanut. What do you think, Tyler?"

"Ms. Peanut!" How could Carrie say that about her beautiful baby?

"Sure." Carrie stifled a giggle, although the stifling wasn't very successful. "Look at her, all wrapped in that blanket. She looks just like a little peanut. No arms, no legs, just a cute little face for one half and..."

"All right, have it your way." Lori couldn't help laughing with Carrie. Tyler got into the act, too, chortling while he put a finger into his sister's fist.

"Look, Mama. She's holding on already. Isn't she smart?"

"Smarter than the rest of us. She's going to sleep while she has the chance." Lori looked over at Carrie. "You want to take her and put her in her bassinet?"

Sheer panic flashed across Carrie's face. "Me? Take her all the way across the room?"

"I think you're up to it." Lori lifted her right

elbow, lifting Mikayla's head as well with her gesture. "She won't break."

Carrie swallowed hard. "If you say so. How do I settle her in that thing?"

"On her back. Just ease your arm out from under there when you get ready to put her down."

Carrie spoke through gritted teeth. "Easy for you to say. I know she's going to wake up when I put her down. Oh, see…" The baby startled a little, then went straight back to sleep. "Okay, maybe not. Maybe I can do this." There was a note of incredulity in Carrie's voice.

"Sure you can. Now come back here and tell me some stuff about what I do next. How much does Tyler know?"

The little boy looked up from where he was driving an imaginary car through the hills and valleys created by Lori's legs under the blanket. "I know lots. What do you want me to know?"

Carrie shook her head. "About his sister, plenty. About the other situation, nothing. And nobody's going to tell him anything, either. Do you have any idea why Mike and I went out there?"

"Not a clue." Lori took a deep breath, trying to sort things out in her mind. "There wasn't more trouble somehow, was there?"

"Just the opposite. The guys do something for Christmas every year, and well, your name came up. I guess Mike and me were the ones who got to…''

''Play Santa Claus.'' So that was why the silly dog was wearing antlers, poor thing. ''But I can't take anything else. That would be worse than ever. Or will it be more paperwork for you if I turn this down?''

Carrie looked skyward. ''Don't even remind me. Sitting in this hospital room is far more pleasant and entertaining than starting my reports.''

''Well, don't get too comfortable. I don't expect to be here too long.'' Lori told her about her situation—the lack of insurance and money needed to stay in the hospital. As she talked, Carrie looked more and more grim.

''That isn't right. I bet there's somebody I can talk to and get that straightened out. Maybe even Mike. I think his mom's on the hospital board.''

Carrie was out of her chair quickly. She might not be confident of her baby-holding skills, but she showed great self-confidence in other areas. Lori wished she could think that fast on her feet.

''No, really, don't do that.'' Didn't she owe Mike enough already? No sense in being beholden to him for one more thing she couldn't pay back.

Carrie wasn't listening. She was already out the door. Tyler pulled on Lori's sleeve. ''Mama? Do we have movies? I'm sleepy. Can we watch movies in bed together and take a nap?''

''I'll find out.'' Lori pushed the call button, preparing herself for the storm that would envelop her when the nurse found out she had a five-year-old for company in her hospital room with no one to take care of him. Maybe nearly giving birth in an ambulance would be the easiest part of her day after all.

''Okay, it's all fixed...'' Mike came into the room talking. He stopped once he crossed the threshold and noticed that nobody was listening to him. Lori and Tyler were both on the bed, cuddled together and asleep. A video played on the TV, sending bright, cheerful cartoon music into the room. A few feet from the bed the top of a swaddled bundle rose and fell in a hospital bassinet.

Mike walked over to look at the baby. She was so beautiful. He saw the card for her name had been filled out at the bottom of the bassinet. Mikayla Hope. Ouch. Why did Lori have to saddle such a beautiful baby with that first name? He wasn't even sure *he* liked Michael after all these years. It still felt funny much of the time, as if it ought to be something else that was just beyond the tip of his tongue.

He'd talked about changing his name as a teenager, but his mom had protested. Every teenager hated their name. And everyone that changed it legally had regrets, according to her. Maybe she was right. When he thought about his high school classmates, almost all of them had reverted to their given names by their recent ten-year reunion. All but Sunshine Feathers. And he couldn't blame her a bit.

There was noise behind him. Mike turned around to see Tyler slip off the bed. "Hey, Mike. That's my baby sister. That's Mikayla Hope."

"I see." Mike motioned to the name tag on the end of the bed. "Her name's written right here."

"Yeah? That says Mikayla Hope? Cool. Does it say anything about me?" Tyler looked at the card. "I don't think so, 'cause I don't see a big *T* anyplace."

"You know your name starts with that big *T*. Pretty smart guy." Mike ruffled the kid's blond hair. It felt good under his hand, almost as good as Lori's would feel. He pulled back his hand. Now why was he making that comparison? He had no right to put a hand in Lori Harper's hair. He would never have that right. No sense in even thinking about it.

"Hey, you guys, don't wake her up," came a sleepy voice from the bed.

"Don't worry. I know that much." Mike crossed

the room and sat in the bedside chair. Tyler
launched himself onto Mike's lap. "So how's the
patient?"

"Good, I think. I needed the sleep. What time is
it?"

"A little after one. You hungry?"

Lori nodded. "Starved. I don't know if I could
really eat if there was food in front of me, but I'm
starved. Does that make any sense?"

"It does, actually. I can remember times after a
fire when I was so hungry, I couldn't think straight.
I also didn't have the energy to lift a burger to my
mouth once I stopped for one. And I imagine giving
birth is a lot harder than putting out a fire."

Lori laughed. "I don't know about that. It is
plenty of work. Is that what you do? Work for fire-
and-rescue?"

"Only volunteer. Dogg and I are part of the
search team when they need us. Mostly he chases
goats and I help manage the family property rental
business."

"Oh."

"I know. It doesn't have nearly the excitement
level as putting out fires. But that's okay most of
the time."

Lori colored. "I didn't mean to put down the
family business…"

"Good, because I think it's about to come in

handy. I don't think you're going to have to go back to that trailer in the middle of nowhere.''

"I'm not? Why?" She sat up straighter. Great. She was going to argue with him.

"Because I've got a better idea, and I'm sure it will be okay with my mother. She's the other half of the property business. When I tell her I found the right client for the property she's most finicky about, she'll thank me.''

"Not when you tell her the client can't pay any rent.'' Lori's chin stuck out defiantly. "I can't let you do this.''

"And I can't let you go back to that place alone with no phone, a five-year-old and a day-old baby.'' Mike tried to keep from shouting. Surely she would listen to reason.

"You can, and will, let me do anything I want. It's not like you're responsible for me or anything.''

"I feel like I am." Why did she have to be so defensive? Why couldn't she just thank him and be grateful? "Besides, this is property that adjoins our home. A lot of times we've rented it out to somebody who either farms a chunk of ground behind both places where my mom doesn't run her goofy herd of Nubian goats, or who can come in and do some of the heavy cleaning and stuff.''

Lori brightened. "Well, I don't know a thing about farming, but I sure can clean."

"Yeah, well, we'll see about that. Not for a month or two anyway."

Lori laughed at him. "A month or two! Do you really think giving birth is that strenuous?"

Mike felt himself blushing. "I don't know. On TV and in the movies, the women always look so fragile, and lie in bed..."

"Not me, my friend. I'm too young to do that."

"And too alone."

Lori shook her head. "No, not alone. The Lord is always with me."

Mike just barely controlled a snort of derision. "Some help He is. If it was up to the Lord you would have given birth in that trailer with Tyler for company."

"Nah..." Tyler's answer surprised him. Mike had forgotten the boy on his lap was probably paying attention to the conversation. "Remember what I told you? Mom said you were her miracle. That means God sent you, silly. He doesn't leave us alone, right, Mom?"

Lori smiled. Mike kept the rest of his opinions to himself on the subject. All he knew is that if God had sent Lori Harper a miracle, He would have done a lot better than him. "Whatever. Can I really not convince you to move in to the house next door to ours?''

Lori's smooth forehead wrinkled. ''It's tempting. I don't really want to go back out to the middle of nowhere, especially now. And I could do that heavy cleaning you talked about, probably by next week.''

''Oh, no. We're not going to go there for a while. Just having somebody in the house will make Mom feel better. She is sure somebody's going to break in over there when it's empty. Kids partying or something.''

''And a widow with two babies is so much better than kids partying.''

Tyler looked up. ''I'm not a baby. An' what's a widow?''

Lori got paler and swallowed hard. ''Oh, boy. Here comes the hard part. Ty, come up here on my bed, okay?''

''Okay.'' He slid off Mike's lap, taking his warmth with him. Mike didn't know what to do next. Did he stay, to give Lori support? Or would it be better if he slipped out of the room to let her do this alone? He tried to convey his confusion without saying anything. Lori wasn't watching. She was reaching out a hand to stroke her son's blond hair.

''He looks so grown up after the baby. But not

grown up enough for this.'' There was a pain in the depth of her eyes that Mike could only imagine.

Is this what his mother's face had looked like when she broke similar news to him? He hadn't been much older than Tyler when his dad died.

"Mind if I stick around?'' It took him a moment to force out the words. "I kind of have some experience here. From Tyler's perspective.''

"How old were you?''

"Six.'' It all came rushing back. At least Tyler wouldn't have the guilt Mike had borne for years. At six he was sure he'd killed his own father. It had taken years more maturity than a first grader possessed to know that his father's fatal heart attack hadn't been Mike's fault.

Tyler cocked his head. He was an astute little kid, and he knew something was going on. "Where's Daddy? When we looked at that place where some of the new babies were, when Carrie was bringing me up here, there were some other kids looking. They were all looking with their dads.''

"That's what we need to talk about.'' Lori stroked his hair again. "Remember when Carrie came this summer? With the truck and the other guy?''

"Mr. Bart? Yeah. He was cool. He let me play with the siren.''

Lori swallowed hard. "That's right. And remember they told us something about Daddy? Something I tried to tell you?" Mike could hear her voice shake.

"Right. That he wasn't coming back. But last time he went away it was different. You said he wasn't coming back for a long time, but then he did. Isn't he coming back to see Mikayla?"

"No, Tyler, he isn't. Not the way you mean it. Daddy had an accident on the way to work. His car went into a lake, and he couldn't get out by himself."

Tyler looked at him, and Mike felt his heart make an elevator ride to his shoes. "Did you help get him out? You and Carrie?"

Mike leaned forward. "No, Tyler, we didn't. We got there too late to help him get out."

"Daddy's dead, Tyler."

"Like Max?"

"A little like Max." "A puppy," Lori mouthed in Mike's direction. "It will be like Max because Daddy won't come home again. The part of him that made him walk and talk and be Daddy isn't here anymore. Being dead means he went to heaven to be with Jesus."

That wasn't an assumption Mike would have made about Gary Harper, but Mike forgave Lori for the fib. After all, this was Harper's kid.

"Do you think Max bited him when he got there?"

"No, I think they're friends. In heaven nobody remembers the bad things you did," Lori said simply.

"So Daddy's still in heaven with Max and Jesus? Can we call him on the phone there?"

"No, Tyler, we can't." Lori was fighting tears now.

Tyler looked puzzled. "Last time he went away, we could talk to him on the phone."

"That's true. But this time is different."

This was raising a lot of questions. Mike felt an ache in his chest at what Lori was facing. "I think I'd better leave both of you alone for a while. Can I go talk to my mom about the house?"

Lori looked up from the bed. "I think you'd better. I'm going to need more help than I thought. Maybe you're going to be the answer to a prayer twice in one day, Mike."

The answer to a prayer? It was the first time he'd ever been called that. Mike wasn't sure it fit. But looking at the glowing eyes of the young woman in the room, he was willing to be the answer to any of her prayers. He'd never been part of a miracle before. But for somebody like Lori, trying to explain the finality of death to a child too young to understand, he could try. She needed all the miracles she could get.

Chapter Four

Mike rehearsed his speech to his mother while he drove home. It earned him a few strange looks from Dogg, who sat in the cab of the truck with his head tilted sideways. True, he'd told Lori everything was worked out and Mom would be fine with her renting the house next door. Now he just had to make sure of that.

He pulled into the drive that circled the house. Parking the truck in his accustomed spot off to the side, where he could pull out any time night or day that a volunteer fire call sounded, he held the door open until Dogg leapt down. He still looked mightily relieved to be rid of those antlers.

"Wipe your feet," he told the beast as they both entered the kitchen. Dogg looked as tired as he did, except the animal's tongue was hanging out farther. Still, he didn't have to worry about the dog's manners; Mike swore Dogg was better about neatness indoors than he was.

The kitchen smelled wonderful. There had to be either veal stew or beef Stroganoff in that pot on the stove for Christmas Eve dinner to make his nose twitch like this. *My mother loves me* was his first thought. She showed it in a variety of ways, but as a savvy woman, Gloria Martin knew how to get to her son through his stomach.

"Hey," Mike called through the house, knowing where he'd find her anyway, even on Christmas Eve.

"Hey, yourself." Gloria was in stocking feet, black pantsuit made festive by an enameled pin in the shape of a holly sprig. As she stood up from the desk in her office, Mike marveled that this tiny woman had borne a big brute like him, and put up with him for all these years.

"I was beginning to think we had to call out the search party. Except you usually *are* the search party, so that didn't leave me with many options." Her red lipstick was unsmudged even this late in the day. Her lacquered nails were the same glossy red. She looked the picture of the successful middle-aged woman.

Mike shrugged. "Well, we had plenty to do. Remember that water rescue we did in August? The department decided his widow should be our Santa Claus case this year. When we went to tell her, we nearly delivered a baby that was a surprise to everybody involved except the mother.''

Gloria's hand flew to her mouth. ''So what will that woman do? Are there other children? And didn't you tell me that man was a drug dealer? Obviously there's no insurance or anything...''

Mike knew his job would be far easier now. ''There's another kid, a little boy about five. He and his mom and his new sister are all as well as can be expected. And as far as what they're going to do now, I think I solved that, as well.''

Gloria's eyes narrowed. ''You rented them the house in back, didn't you, Michael? Or knowing you, the use of the house has been promised, but this woman has no hope of paying rent.''

''Got it in one, Mom. She does promise to do the heavy cleaning. In fact if it was up to her, I think Lori would be doing the heavy cleaning before the first of the year.''

Gloria's artfully tinted brown curls bounced as she shook her head. ''Not that soon. I'm glad you did it, Mike. It will be good to have children around. Especially since I seem destined to be without grandchildren until I am too old and feeble to hold them.''

Mike scowled. "Okay, it's Christmas Eve. We are not going to get into that tonight. You going to open your present before supper or after?"

"After." Gloria laughed. "It's not even dark yet. I don't open presents before dark on Christmas Eve. And you need a shower before dinner anyway. Go wash up and come back presentable."

"Okay, but no decorating Dogg while I'm gone. He's had enough of that today."

"Not even one plaid bow?"

Mike sighed. "If he'll let you put it on, you can do that. And of course you can brush him. But no jingle bells or pine roping or anything."

His mother gave a very unladylike snort behind him. "Pine roping. Who does he think I am?" Even though he was headed out of the room, Mike already knew that Dogg's big head was in her small hands. They both loved the attention. "You'd *eat* pine roping. And mistletoe is poisonous, so we can't have you wearing that, either. Let's go find that plaid ribbon, the one with the gold edges, shall we?" Mike heard the sound of Dogg's nails ticking down the hardwood hallway as they both went their separate ways to prepare for Christmas Eve.

An hour later they were all in the dining portion of the big country kitchen. Mike tried to disguise his exhaustion with aftershave and a bright red sweater. It might work, depending on how close Mom was paying attention.

There were candles everywhere there was flat space in the kitchen. It did seem kind of quiet, just two people and one dog, even if he took up more floor space than one of the people. Maybe his mom was right about the lack of grandchildren. A few rug rats would definitely spice up the holidays. Of course he'd have to meet the right woman first. One that would pass muster with his mother, as well as being able to put up with all his foibles. And it wouldn't hurt if she were soft and small and easy on the eyes, too. That would take another couple of decades at least.

As a special treat, Dogg got a little veal stew on top of his kibble. He inhaled his food and stretched out on the rug with a sigh. Mike ate in silence for a while, then pushed back from his place. "I'm probably going back to the hospital tomorrow to get Lori. She and the baby are both healthy, and I expect they'll be ready to discharge her by noon. She doesn't have much in the way of insurance and there's nobody she can stay with."

"She'll need people around. Don't take her straight to that empty house. Bring her here and I'll stretch out Christmas dinner."

Jumping up from the table and hugging his mom felt like a good idea right now. But that would not be Gloria's idea of good dinner decorum. Better to stay seated. "Great. I can't thank you enough for being understanding about this. I know I don't usually bring fire-and-rescue home with me, but this time something was different."

"I'm glad you're reacting this way. I can honestly say I've been where this young woman is, and it's not a pretty place to be." Gloria looked down at her plate. As usual she'd stirred around a small portion of dinner, hardly seeming to eat.

"At least you had money to fall back on. I don't think there's any there." Mike looked at his mother. Did he dare ask a question he'd wondered about for years? Hey, it was Christmas. Why not? "And you just had me. Did you ever regret that I was an only child?"

Gloria's smile was crooked. "All the time. Except maybe that year your dad died. Then I was thankful I didn't have any littler ones to deal with. You were a little old man by then, so serious. I couldn't imagine having a baby or a toddler in that situation."

"Well, try a five-year-old, a baby, one junker car that I could see out there in the middle of nowhere and only the possessions that fill a very small mobile home that ceased to be mobile during the Nixon administration."

Gloria actually grimaced. "Definitely bring her

here. I wonder if there was any Christmas for the little boy.''

"No idea. I pretty much doubt it.'' Sitting there contemplating the Harpers' Christmas made his head hurt. "Could we have coffee and some of those Christmas cookies I know are on that tray on the countertop? I feel like I've been run over by a truck all of a sudden.''

Gloria got up briskly and cleared the plates before Mike could move. Putting them next to the sink, she flipped the switch on the coffeepot, which hummed to life. "I had it all set up. I figured the day would catch up to you sooner or later.'' She walked over to him at the table and massaged his shoulders. Her hands were so fine boned. "Think you'll still be awake when the carolers come?''

"Only if they make it in the next half hour. Otherwise I'm joining Dogg under the tree so we can look up at the pretty blinking lights.''

Gloria looked at the bubbling pot. "I should have brewed more coffee.'' Even as tired as he was, Mike had to laugh. His mother was ever the hostess. Even with just the two of them there on Christmas Eve.

"Hey, for your sake I'll try to stay awake until at least nine. And then we'll open gifts. Can Dogg unwrap his this year?''

Gloria made a face. "Only if you feel like vacuuming before you go to bed.'' His mother loved him. But she was definitely still the mother he'd grown up with. Somehow that gave Mike more comfort than if she would have said yes to his goofy request.

"C'mon, Dogg, let's go plug in those tree lights." The big beast's ears perked up and he padded behind Mike into the living room, where they could both take an after-dinner nap.

Gloria liked her bracelet. Of course, she would have professed to like anything Mike gave her if he'd picked it out himself. But Mike could tell once she'd seen the delicate serpentine gold chain with its Victorian slide charms that she approved. It went on immediately with several exclamations.

Dogg helped unwrap his present after all. He could smell the basted rawhide bones through the package, and nosed his way into Mike's lap to help with the paper. "Take that into the kitchen," Gloria cautioned him. Mike didn't bother answering because he knew she was speaking directly to the dog. And he listened, too. One prized bone in his mouth, it never touched the carpet in his trek to the right spot on the woven rag rug in front of the sink.

"Aren't you going to open yours?"

"Sure." Mike eyed the box. "Bet I can guess what it is anyway."

Gloria shook her head. "I bet you can't."

It was on the tip of Mike's tongue to describe in detail the baseball jacket he expected. Surely it was there in red splendor, complete with the number 25 of his favorite St. Louis Cardinals player.

But something held him back. That was his fantasy. His mom was not likely to know that's what he'd been looking at in store windows, nor believe the kind of money to be spent on such foolishness, at least in her eyes. One look back at Dogg decked out in gold-edged plaid told Mike he was going to be vastly disappointed if he expected that jacket.

So while he unfastened the neatly taped edges of the paper, he rearranged his expectations. It was easier than asking to exchange a present from Gloria. When he opened the bulky box, there was a jacket inside. A beautiful salt-and-pepper herringbone tweed in soft wool. He didn't even have to look inside to know that it was the 46 long he wore. "All right." He held up the garment, trying to inject as much enthusiasm as he could into the statement. "This is some jacket."

"You'd been hinting about needing a new one. If it doesn't fit, you'll have to go into St. Louis to exchange it, because nobody around here had anything nearly good enough."

They wouldn't, not for Gloria. "Thanks, Mom." Mike got up and went to her chair, leaning down to kiss her cheek. "I'm sure it will fit, though." It would also hang in his closet about twenty-nine days out of thirty until he was escorting his mother to some business-related function, but he wouldn't bring that up.

"I think I'll call it a night. Guess I'm going to miss those carolers after all."

"You do look tired. Merry Christmas, dear."

"Merry Christmas." It sounded hollow somehow. And once he was in his room stretched out on his bed, sleep wasn't quick in coming. He was exhausted. How could he not sleep? Easy. All he had to do was take his imagination across town to the hospital. Up to the third floor to where he knew a young woman was probably staring at a ceiling with the same intensity he was.

After half an hour Mike surrendered. He picked up the cordless phone on the bedside table and punched in the numbers of the hospital. The switchboard was long closed and he got the long series of recorded instructions. While he listened to them drone on, he cast about frantically in his memory for Lori's room number.

Finally at the point where the recorded message was repeating itself and he was sure he didn't remember the number, it popped into his head and he punched it in. One ring, then two. What if it wasn't the right number? He had this vision of waking up somebody that had finally taken his or her sleeping pill and drifted off.

"Hello?" That was Lori's voice, wasn't it?

"Lori?"

"Yes." She sounded puzzled. But then, Mike reasoned, the woman had no family around here, and precious few friends. It was probably kind of odd to get a call in the middle of the night in the hospital, on Christmas.

"It's Mike. Mike Martin. I couldn't sleep, and I wondered how things were going. I woke you up, didn't I?"

"No, you didn't. We've got Tyler on this cool fold-out recliner thing, and he's sound asleep. Mikayla is in her bassinet, and she's asleep too. She's fun to watch sleep, Mike. I'd forgotten what kind of squinchy little noises newborns make. They squeak."

There was a touch of laughter in her voice. Mike marveled at it. How could somebody go through everything Lori had, and still be able to laugh about squeaky babies?

"Now that I'm talking to you, I have no idea why I called." It felt better admitting it. "I'll let you get to sleep like your kids."

"No, I'm glad you called. I was lying here doing the craziest thing. You'll think I'm even stranger than you do already, but I was connecting the dots on the ceiling tile.''

"What do yours make? Our house has this textured ceiling paint, and in my bedroom there's a rabbit. Or a llama or something.''

"Lucky you. Best I've come up with is an amoeba.''

"That's one ugly ceiling.'' And one strange conversation. But somehow it was comforting. "So do you think they'll still let you out before noon?''

"Looks like it. Everybody's healthy, and the nurses have been so sweet about keeping Tyler here. Not that there's much of an alternative, unless we talk about temporary foster care. And nobody wanted to do that to us at Christmas, thank heavens.''

"And you'll let us bring you here?''

Lori sighed. "I will. I hate to take charity from total strangers, but watching Mikayla sleep has been the last straw. I can't go back out to the country, with no phone, a car that only starts when it wants to and this tiny baby. But I *am* going to be doing that housecleaning by next week.''

"Next year. That could be after next week.'' Or it could be in a couple months, like spring, when Mike might feel more ready to let this pixie of a woman clean anything in his mother's house.

"We'll see.'' She was quite a determined pixie.

There was a pause for a moment. "I did think of one thing we need tomorrow. Do you have access to a car seat?"

Now that had him stumped. It took a minute for the reality of this to sink in. He was bringing home a real, live newborn baby. On Christmas Day. "I'll call Carrie. I'm pretty sure fire-and-rescue loans them out to parents who don't have one, so that nobody goes home from the hospital without. Besides, she'll love getting a call about six in the morning on Christmas Day."

"You hound. Wait until at least eight or nine when she's up. I think single people sleep in past daylight on holidays."

"Maybe. I still think I'd have more fun my way."

"For about ten minutes. Then she'd be figuring out ways to murder you, wouldn't she?"

Mike had to laugh. "Yeah, she would. Even Carrie isn't a good enough friend that she'd let me get away with that. Hey, I had one other question. What's the Santa situation for a certain young man asleep in your room?"

"Not real great, I'm afraid." There was sadness in her voice. "I haven't exactly had the time or the money to go out and get much. Especially with him tagging along. He'd figure things out pretty quickly if toys that showed up in a shopping cart he was sitting in came from Santa.''

''True. There's a lot to this kid business that I have to learn.'' Mike's own statement stopped him cold. He didn't know anything about kids, except what he remembered from being one. And that was pretty sketchy. But how he wanted to learn, for Lori's sake, and maybe for his own.

This was getting way too deep with somebody he'd only met this morning. Lori must have thought so, too, because she hadn't said anything for a while. ''Hey, I'll let you go. Want me to call in the morning before I come by to get you?''

''Please. Tell the rabbit good-night for me.''

Huh? Oh, yeah. The rabbit on the ceiling. ''Will do. And you tuck in that amoeba.'' Mike hung up. This was way, way too deep already. And he knew things could only get deeper. Why wasn't that bothering him?

Chapter Five

Carrie found a car seat. And two stuffed animals from the ambulance supply that they gave to transported kids. And a bright shiny red fire truck that Mike suspected came from somebody's private stock, meant for a son or nephew. Fire and rescue folks were generous that way.

Tyler had no problem believing that Santa made a drop-off at Carrie's house when jolly old Saint Nick found out he wasn't home. It made perfect sense to him that his toys would find him, no matter what.

The fire truck was an instant hit. Stuffed animals were okay, and got a few seconds of perusal before being put down. But Mike could see that the kid was probably going to sleep with that fire truck before he let go of it. That small thing meant a lot to him. Kids were so resilient.

He could see the thanks in Lori's eyes. Of course she couldn't say anything out loud without giving away the game. Carrie had also brought a fluffy pink receiving blanket and some amazingly tiny sleepers for Mikayla. "She looks like an elf." Carrie settled a matching pointed hat on the sleeping baby. "Doesn't she, Mike?"

She actually looked like a red, squashy baby to him, but he suspected admitting that would be trouble. Silence was probably the best route here. He smiled, hoping to look sincere. "Can I carry anything down to the truck?"

"Not much to carry." Lori looked around the room. She had her hospital supplies, issued on admission, and a bag that must have contained yesterday's outfit. It was then Mike realized that what he'd taken for a relatively attractive matching shirt and pants were hospital scrubs lent to her by a nurse. Even a day after giving birth she managed to make the outfit look like tailored separates.

"I'm sorry," he blurted out. "We were so busy getting stuff for Tyler and the baby. I didn't think about you."

Lori shrugged. "I thought about calling Carrie, to have her go by the trailer, but then I realized I didn't have a phone number for her at home."

"You could have called me."

Her snub nose wrinkled. "I most certainly could not have called you. I needed girl stuff, mister. It's one thing to horn in on somebody's Christmas dinner. It's a whole 'nother ball game to ask a strange man to go through your underwear drawer."

Mike could feel the color rising from his collar. "I see what you mean. Do you want to stop by there on the way home?"

Lori shook her head. "I'd like to, but I don't think I'm up to it."

"Let me," Carrie said firmly. She was carrying a bag full of hospital supplies, bringing up the rear in the parade down the hall. A nurse pushed the wheelchair with Lori and Mikayla in it, while Mike followed behind with Tyler and his fire engine.

There wasn't much activity in the hospital on Christmas Day. Everybody who could possibly go home had gone. Carrie insisted on being the one to go by the trailer, over Lori's protests. "You have a family, and it's Christmas. We can make do until tomorrow, and then I can get Mike or his mom to take me over there, I'm sure."

Carrie wouldn't be swayed. "My family is very understanding. And there isn't that much family. They're used to postponing holiday dinners because of my crazy schedule anyway. How often do you think I get a whole day off even on Christmas?''

"That's probably true. Let me give you the key." Lori giggled as she fished through her battered pocketbook. "I hope I remembered to lock up. We were kind of in a hurry."

"You might say that." Carrie's eyes sparkled. "It was worth the rush, wasn't it?"

"Definitely." They both looked down at the bundle in Lori's arms.

Mike still didn't get it. She was probably real pretty, for a baby less than a day old. But the two women seemed infatuated by her to a degree he couldn't understand. The nurse joined them in their cooing. He looked at Tyler.

Here he had an ally. The boy shrugged his shoulders and held on to his fire engine. "Must be a girl thing," he said softly. Mike held back laughter as the elevator opened to let them out in the lobby of the hospital.

He discovered it wasn't a universal girl thing when he brought everybody home. Gloria met them at the door. She was warm to Lori, and made noises over the baby. But Tyler was definitely the man she wanted to talk to.

Mike didn't complain. Her attention to Tyler and his shiny new fire engine gave them time to get Lori settled on the leather couch in the family room, setting the infant seat beside her. Dogg padded up to greet her, sniffing the baby gently, then putting one large paw on Lori's knee.

"Yes, she's mine. That's what all the hurry was about yesterday." Lori stroked his pointed ears and Mike watched his big, tough dog melt. "Don't you look festive."

"Mom's doing. I do not put plaid ribbon on Dogg, no matter what the occasion." Lori would probably think the dog would look cute with ribbons. It just wasn't a guy thing, though. "Can I get you something before dinner? Eggnog or anything?"

Lori shook her head. "No eggnog. I'd take a cup of tea if you can handle that."

"I can handle that. Boiling water is my specialty."

She had a great laugh. "Good. Boil a whole pot of it then. Sitting here on this couch with Mikayla and a pot of tea is my idea of a lovely Christmas Day."

Mike wanted to tell her she didn't have very high standards. Christmas Day, or any other day, ought to be made up of better moments than just parking on the couch with the baby and a pot of tea. Then he took a minute to review what he knew about Lori.

She was the only adult in charge at her place.

And *place* was being nice. There was no leather sofa in that mobile home, no crackling fire across the room and certainly no one to make her a pot of tea. So maybe he better keep his mouth shut and boil water.

Lori looked around the family room of the Martins' house. She had never seen so much comfort in one place in her life. The furniture was plush upholstery or burnished leather. The fireplace took up nearly one wall in brick and stone, flanked by wood bookcases that held more books than she'd ever owned. Maybe more than she'd checked out of libraries in a lifetime.

So this was how the other half lived. Gary had always phrased things that way, and Lori had never taken it in until now. This kind of luxury, which her hosts took totally for granted, was what Gary had meant. It was what he wanted to provide for them, even if he went about it in a warped manner.

Gary had always been working and scheming so that they could see how the other half lived. But she had been happy with the way they were living. Especially for that brief time early on when Gary was still in school and she had dropped out to work to bring in money. She would have kept at it, too, even after Tyler was born. Surely between the two of them they could have worked out a schedule. By then she was the assistant manager at the Kwik Stop and she could have taken the undesirable night hours herself for more money. But Gary wouldn't hear of it.

No wife of his was going to work, not with a new baby. He would quit school and be the breadwinner. Unfortunately the jobs he was qualified for with only two years of a four-year science degree didn't pay as well as her job at the Kwik Stop.

How different would life be for all of them right now if she could have convinced him that God really fulfilled all their needs? Was she really such a mutant for believing in those promises? Everyone around her seemed to think so. Gary certainly had. And look where it had led him.

Trusting himself to provide for his family without any help from God, Gary Harper was dead before he turned twenty-eight. He'd done time in jail for using that half a chemistry degree to make illegal drugs. And never once during the time he was alive did he really get to see how the other half lived.

It was so sad. Lori looked around the room again. Her tea would get cold if she mused much longer about this. And Mike had gone to a lot of trouble. He'd found one of his mom's good teapots—Lori was sure there was more than one in a house like this. The one on the table beside her was heavy English stoneware in a Christmasy green. A matching mug sat beside it. Nothing was chipped or dented here.

Lori felt like shaking her head. If this was what Gary had been after, he shouldn't have bothered. The Martins had a beautiful home. Fine furniture was everywhere, and even the dog was decorated for Christmas. But somehow there was an emptiness that made Lori miss the trailer.

As the afternoon progressed, she grew even more uncomfortable. Mike's mom was serving an excellent dinner off more matching china and silver than Lori had ever seen outside a department store. There was even Christmas-print cloth napkins, which Tyler had to be instructed on using. He'd never seen a napkin that didn't come in a paper package of three hundred.

But there was so much missing. Dinner wasn't over yet, and she could already feel the tension building in her. Tyler was going to pipe up with a comment any minute that would dampen the lovely atmosphere, and there wasn't anything she could do to stop him.

"Hey, guy, you ready for dessert?" Here it came. Mike's innocent question was going to set off the firestorm. Lori looked at him, trying to warn him of what might be coming, but no such luck. He was looking at Tyler, who was a sight.

"Sure. It's Christmas. My favorite." Tyler was grinning so wide, he looked like a jack-o'-lantern. Where he was going to put dessert after that much turkey and ham and green-bean casserole was a mystery.

"Mine, too." Lori tried again to catch Mike's eye, warn him somehow that he and Tyler weren't on the same track. Before she could do that, Mikayla woke up and it was time to take her in the other room for her own dinner.

"Need any help?" Lori could tell the words were a reflex for Mike. He was used to helping women around this house.

"No, I think I'm on my own for this one." Lori tried to hide a grin at his blush.

"Yeah, I guess so."

"I could use a big glass of water." Lori remembered this part from Tyler's first few months. She needed to get into the habit of drinking something every time Mikayla nursed.

"Sure." Mike was up in a flash. He settled the tumbler of water at her elbow as she got comfortable leaning on the arm of the leather sofa in the family room. Carrie's fluffy receiving blanket made a nice tent for the baby. "This still looks like magic to me."

"Not magic. Maybe a little miracle. But one that sure happens for a lot of people."

"I guess." Mike looked across the long room into the kitchen where his mother was working on a dessert tray. "What was baby feeding like nearly thirty years ago? This must be a familiar picture."

Gloria looked startled. "Heavens. I didn't ever... I mean, you..."

"Nursing wasn't too fashionable for a while, Michael. Even the doctors didn't push it much," Lori said. Gloria gave her a grateful look, as if she'd saved her from something. It was puzzling. The whole exchange made Lori wonder, but the thought was there and gone so fast, she lost it.

"Definitely." If Lori knew her hostess better, she would say that was relief in the older woman's voice. "Everybody bottle fed. Mostly that lovely soy formula. I remember my friend Helen saying she never did get the spit-up stains out of her favorite chair."

"Charming." Mike headed back to the table. "I'm so glad I asked."

Lori could hear Mike and Tyler help clear the table, with lots of clanging and rattling in their help. Mike didn't seem much more gentle with his mom's good china than Tyler.

Coward that she was, she urged them not to wait for her for dessert. Maybe Tyler would keep quiet if he didn't have her to make faces at.

Then Gloria brought her delicately arranged tray

to the table. Here it came. "Oh. Cookies." Tyler's voice sounded flat, even to Lori.

"Sure. What did you expect?" Mike sounded puzzled. Even without seeing him Lori knew his broad forehead was wrinkling.

"Birthday cake. And ice cream." Tyler's scornful tone told everyone listening that any idiot knew that.

"Isn't that for your birthday, Tyler?" Gloria's voice was gentle but confused. Lori wanted to blurt something out to stop Tyler from his reply. He was much too young to know that his innocent beliefs might hurt someone else's feelings, or make them uncomfortable. And after all that Mike and his mother had done for them already, challenging their beliefs was the last thing Lori wanted.

"Yeah, that's for my birthday. It's the only other time we have it. Then on Christmas we have birthday cake and ice cream again, for Jesus. I guess having cookies means we're not going to sing 'Happy Birthday,' either. I like telling Jesus happy birthday."

The table was silent. Then Lori could hear Gloria stifle a giggle. "Birthday cake for the baby Jesus. Now why didn't I ever think of that?"

There were footsteps on the polished parquet, then a soft smack. Without even looking around the corner, Lori knew Tyler's reaction to being kissed.

He had to be rubbing whatever portion of his head or face had gotten Gloria's lipstick kiss. "I can't whip up a cake on this short notice, Tyler. But there's chocolate ice cream in the kitchen freezer. And we can definitely sing 'Happy Birthday.' Now come and help me scoop, okay?"

"Okay!" The thump of Tyler's tennis shoes hitting the floor was followed by him racing across the room.

"Walk in the house," Lori called out as loudly as she dared without waking Mikayla. The baby was back to sleep, satisfied and full now. And it was Lori who felt foolish.

Tyler hadn't embarrassed anybody. Like always, he trusted God in his childlike way, and said what was on his mind. So now he was getting his chocolate ice cream and they would all sing "Happy Birthday."

Maybe how the other half lived wasn't so different after all. Lori settled her daughter back in the infant seat. Chocolate ice cream sounded pretty good. And Gloria looked like a good substitute for the doting grandmother she'd always wished Tyler could have. And then there was Mike, already working his way into her heart in so many ways. "Thank you. And happy birthday," she whispered. It was a quick prayer, but a heartfelt one.

Chapter Six

Okay, what did they do now? Mike stared into the fire wondering how to handle having strangers spend the tail end of Christmas Day. This was one time when he wished his mom hadn't converted to gas logs. He had nothing to stir around, and no reason to go outside for wood.

How did they all stay comfortable? Tyler's "birthday party" had kept things going for a while. But now the fire was dying, it was getting dark outside and the dishes were done. Christmas Day had just about run out of steam.

Tyler was stretched out on the couch with Dogg's big head on one knee. Maybe he could take the two of them for a walk, if the kid had a coat. It would burn off some excess energy.

Mike looked at Lori, sitting in the chair where she had nursed Mikayla earlier. She was asleep sitting up. It had to have been a rough day for her. This was the first Christmas without her husband, and her first full day of being the mother of two. He couldn't even imagine how much pressure that put on a little thing like her.

The baby was sleeping in her infant seat. She was so tiny. Definitely getting better looking as the day passed. Time was making her look less red and squashy. She was still awful pink. But that nose was getting some shape, was maybe going to be pug like her mom's. What color were her eyes? Or did all newborn babies have kind of bluish eyes like kittens? It was a good question, one he had no answer to.

He wasn't going to wake Lori up to ask her. The nap would be over soon enough anyway. Naps always were, even on Christmas. Mike moved in his chair and Dogg perked up in response. His big brush tail thumped the floor, hoping for some more attention. He was getting plenty from Tyler, but there was always hope in his canine heart for more.

Mike knew how he felt. There had been plenty of times in his life where he felt the same way. Were other people satisfied with the attention they got? Was that feeling of yearning for that mental pat on the head something unique to him and Dogg? Surely not.

As he thought, Mike watched Dogg. His ears perked up even more, and he slipped from under Tyler's hand, heading to the front hall. When he got about halfway to the door, the bell rang.

Mike got up to answer it before the noise of barking and company in the hall could wake up everyone. Carrie stood in the doorway with a paper bag in her hands and a troubled expression.

"Hey. What's up?" Something was wrong. Carrie wasn't that serious unless she was on a call, normally.

She came in and Mike closed the door, shutting out the cold air behind her. Dogg pushed his pointed nose into the underside of her arm, and she let go of the paper bag with one hand to pet him.

"I'm not sure. Help me out with something. Maybe I'm just remembering wrong."

This sounded strange. Carrie was usually the detail person. "Go ahead."

"Yesterday when we were at Lori's trailer, I know you didn't have much time to look around. But how would you describe the place?"

Mike tilted his head back, thinking. "Neat. Clean. Nothing much new, but pretty tidy, especially with a kid living there."

"Okay. That's what I thought, too. Somebody tossed the place since we've been there."

Great. So much for Christmas winding down quietly. "Anything missing? I don't remember much worth taking in there."

"Me, neither. But what was there had been looked through. Drawers dumped on the bed and floor, even in the kid's room. Kitchen cabinets all open and stuff shoved around. Whoever did it was quick. There wasn't a lot of vandalism."

"That's a plus. It means it probably wasn't teenagers out to impress each other."

Carrie nodded. "Nothing broken, no spray paint tagging on the walls. But Lori definitely had company. I hate to be the one to tell her. I mean, doesn't she have enough to deal with already?"

"You'd think." She'd handle this in stride, like everything else. Probably even find some good news in it, like she had everything else. He'd never met anybody else who spent as much time looking for miracles.

Of course she seemed to find them every time, so who was the oddball? Maybe if he looked for more of them, they'd pop up in his life. Right. And maybe Dogg would grow antlers. "Come on back and we'll tell her. She's going to have to go out there to see if anything's missing."

"I know. That's the part I hate, dragging her

over there like this. But I won't feel comfortable unless we make a police report." Carrie grimaced. "They're going to love being called out today, too. It's just my lucky day all around."

"Don't say that in front of Lori. She'll find a reason why it really is."

"Say what in front of me?" Lori's pale blond head rose out of the chair, and she passed the back of one hand across her face in a gesture that nearly broke Mike's heart in its simplicity and innocence.

"That it's Carrie's lucky day. And before you start agreeing, let her tell you why it isn't." Her eyes widened and she sat back in the chair. Mike felt like he'd slapped a puppy, given her reaction, but he wasn't in the mood for any chipper stuff right now. This was serious business for once, and needed to be attended to in a serious way. Then why did he feel so bad? Merry Christmas to all, for sure.

Lori looked at the outside of the trailer. This had been home for over a year. Had it always looked this awful? Somehow she didn't remember it being that banged up or dingy. Maybe just being away from it for a couple of days gave her a new perspective. If so, it wasn't a particularly attractive one.

The concrete block steps up to the door looked

less sturdy than usual. How had she gotten up and down those things the last few weeks? God only knew. Thank heavens she'd had His help and protection. Who knows what would have happened if the robbers, or whoever, had broken in while she and Tyler were there.

"Was the door locked when you got here?" Lori asked. Carrie put her hand on the smooth metal.

She shrugged. "I'm not sure. It took me a while fiddling with the key to get the door to open. But you said it stuck, so I couldn't tell whether I was locking and then unlocking it, or what."

"I always had trouble with that myself. Gary said it didn't matter because we didn't have anything worth stealing. I was more concerned about Tyler getting out at night and going for some big adventure." She shivered at the thought.

Mike was there beside her, a large, steadying arm around her. It felt so good. "You sure you're up to this? Let me at least take the baby." He shifted Mikayla and the infant seat from Lori's hand without disturbing the blanket or the sleeping baby under it. In his hands it looked like such a tiny parcel.

Lori didn't complain. The baby and the seat were heavy, and she knew Mike would be careful with her precious cargo. Already she trusted him, probably more than she should. Still, there were so many things that told her that he had a good heart.

"I have to be. Nobody else could tell you if there's something missing." She pushed off his concern and went into the mobile home. At least the lamp in the living room wasn't broken, and the bulb still worked when she turned the switch.

After standing in the dim light taking everything in, Lori almost wished she hadn't turned on the lamp. Anybody seeing the living room or the kitchen would think she was a terrible housekeeper.

Nothing was in its place. Couch cushions sagged onto the floor. What few magazines had been on the rickety coffee table were torn and scattered. The stacked plastic crates in the corner that held her books and Tyler's toys were in a jumbled heap.

"The kitchen isn't as bad as it could be." Carrie sounded hopeful. It was good of her to try and cheer her up. Lori tried to manage a weak smile. She could feel her lip trembling. Wonderful. Now was not the time to cry. If she'd kept it together during the rest of this crazy, awful day surely she could do it now.

"Let's go see." Her voice sounded firmer than she expected. *Thanks, Lord, for small favors.* In the end, weren't they the kind that mattered most? Those little gifts and blessings that kept you going from moment to moment? And there had been so many of those today and yesterday. Maybe this would be another one somehow.

Hey, God could do anything. Surely the same Being who gave away His only son could be trusted to smooth out her pitiful little problems. Lori took a deep breath and went into the kitchen.

Carrie was right. It could have been worse. None of the dishes were broken, and the few staples on hand had been searched, but not doused with paint or syrup or anything awful. Of course there was precious little to douse in the first place, and the dishes were that hard stuff that was supposed to resist elephants sitting on it. With a five-year-old helping with dishes, that was the only kind that lasted anyway.

"There's nothing missing that I can see in either room." The secondhand TV, a thirteen-inch that just barely pulled in cartoons for Tyler on good days, looked untouched. The boom-box-style radio that she carted from room to room to play his few tapes and listen to the two radio stations she could pull in was still on the kitchen countertop. The tape compartment gaped open, but she might have left it that way herself in the haste to lie down when she went into labor.

Yesterday? Surely that was a lifetime ago. Lori wondered at the changes in thirty-six hours. "Let's look in the bedrooms. Maybe I can do that sitting down."

Mike was at her elbow again. He set down the

infant seat softly on the floor, freeing both hands. "Do you need me to carry you? You're not dizzy or anything?"

"No, everything's just catching up with me. If I could walk to the truck yesterday, I can surely walk around my own house today." Besides, it wouldn't be a good idea to have Mike pick her up. That would definitely distract her from the business at hand. In his arms she would melt. And melting just wasn't on the agenda right now.

Lori made it down the short hallway and into Tyler's room. Every drawer of his dresser was dumped on the floor. What on earth had someone been looking for? The mattress was half off the bed and his blankets strewn about on the floor. Still, nothing was broken or torn.

Her room was much the same. The closet had gotten serious searching. Lori hoped the creep had enjoyed going through her meager possessions. Did he get a real charge out of the silly cardboard box full of memories? The three snapshots that were her wedding pictures? That crumpled envelope that held Tyler's lock of pale blond hair from his first haircut? Whoever had been in here had pawed through it all, for sure.

The history of her life was on her bedroom floor. Lori sat down there and quietly gathered it all up. All the pieces went back into the heavy cardboard box. As she smoothed the last crumpled piece of paper under her hands, she read it. How macabre. It was Gary's death certificate. And how very strange. "This can't be right," she murmured.

"What?" Mike, ever vigilant, was down on the floor beside her. Mikayla stirred a little when he set her down this time, but settled back to sleep, one small foot kicking out under the blanket.

"See here? I didn't see this before. It says 'cause of death: undetermined.' But the officers were very plain about what killed him. They said he ran off the road, the car went into that pond and he drowned."

She looked over at Carrie. "Yesterday I heard something in the E.R. Something about Gary and illegal drugs. Do you think this 'unknown' business could be related to that?"

"I can check on that later if you like. And I'm sorry you heard something like that in any case. But for now we have to get back to what's happening in the trailer." Carrie sounded impatient. "But is there anything missing or broken?"

"Nothing I can see. But I think I want to take this box with me when we go back…to Mike's." She almost said *back home*. Funny how this trailer didn't feel like home in any way. Maybe it never had. It was sort of a way station, like a bus terminal waiting room. "Should we call the police?"

Carrie looked at Mike. He shrugged. "Your call. Somebody's been here, for sure. But the lady says nothing is missing, and nothing has been damaged. Whoever is watch commander is going to be really ticked about bringing somebody out on a holiday for a report that isn't going to go anywhere."

Lori roused herself from thought, still sitting on the floor. "Let's just lock up and go back to Mike's. We can call the police from there tomorrow. We don't need to ruin anybody's Christmas over this."

"Anybody else's, at least." One corner of his mouth turned up. It made Mike look even more boyish and even more appealing, if that was possible. "It probably did a good job on yours."

"Not really. Like we said, nothing is gone or broken. And I don't have a clue what they were looking for. They left me the few things of value." She lifted the box. "I could replace those awful kitchen dishes at a garage sale, but nobody else has a lock of Tyler's hair."

Mike shook his head. He looked like Dogg worrying a bone. "Lady, you are incredible. Let's get you back to the house before you run out of steam."

"More importantly, let's get back before this baby wakes up. She has to be changed and fed again soon, and it would be a lot easier at your house than on the road in Carrie's SUV.''

''Now that's being practical.'' Mike stood up and hefted the infant seat with one hand. He held out the other one to Lori. ''Let's go.''

His outstretched hand with its long fingers looked like a lifeline. She took it and let him help her off the floor. His hand was incredibly warm and the strength that flowed from him engulfed her. This would be so easy. Just to let somebody else take over, do the hard stuff for a while. Especially if that someone was Mike.

No, she still had to be strong. To keep it together, and let God do the managing for her, not some other human being. Or did she? What if Mike is just managing things for God? It was a new thought. Maybe Mikayla Hope wasn't the only miracle here after all.

Maybe God had sent her a trio of guardian angels. Gloria seemed perfectly happy when they left her to haul games out of the basement and play with Tyler while they were gone. That was a gift in itself.

Lori stifled a giggle. It was too much. Thinking about Mike this way, sprouting a halo and wings, was hard enough. But the image that came to mind of a matching set of equipment on Dogg did the trick.

Then Mike cocked his head in puzzlement, much like his canine buddy probably did. That brought on the laughter in earnest. "Yes, let's get going. I think I'm getting a little goofy."

A *little* goofy? Mike didn't say a word, but the look he exchanged with Carrie said it all for him. He obviously thought she'd gone around the bend. Lori let go of his hand and followed him out of the trailer.

This time she was sure they turned off the light and locked the door. If there was any more tampering with the place after this, she would know.

Chapter Seven

Mike stood in his mom's guest room, kicking himself again. Where was this baby going to sleep? How could neither he nor Gloria anticipate that they needed a crib or a bassinet? Him, he could understand. Mikayla was the first baby he'd ever been this close to. It was natural that he wouldn't know what they'd need. But why hadn't his mom thought of this?

Lori picked up on it immediately. "Now what's the matter?"

He shrugged. "No crib. I don't know what I thought you were going to do with the baby. Put her in your pouch like a kangaroo, I guess. She can't sleep in that thing all night." He motioned toward the infant seat Mikayla still occupied. She'd fallen asleep on the ride home from the trailer, and slept peacefully. At least she was unaware of the lack of preparation that had been made for her.

"She could if she needed to." Lori looked around the room. "What do you think I was going to do with her back there? Did you see a crib?"

"Come to think of it, no. What were you going to do with her?"

"The same thing I did with Tyler. Watch." Lori set the seat down on the carpet and walked over to the antique dresser with all the little porcelain what-nots on it. How his mom ever dusted all this stuff, and why she would want to, was beyond him. It was her guest room, though, so if she wanted to put all this froufrou in it, that was no skin off his nose.

Lori opened the lowest drawer and set it on the floor. She took out the sewing patterns and other contents then removed the scented drawer liner paper. At least that was what the stuff printed with violets seemed to be. Mike didn't know until now they made such a product, much less that anybody bought it. However now that he was aware that somebody made it, there was no surprise in knowing his mother used it.

He watched as Lori folded one of Mikayla's blankets into a rectangle that fit the drawer. "See? Instant crib. Folks have been doing it this way for generations. In fact, as old as this dresser is, it was probably used this way before.''

"I don't know about that. Martin babies have probably had hand-carved cradles for generations.'' As soon as Mike said that, he wondered. If that was the case, where was that cradle? If Gloria had been in possession of such an item, surely she would have hauled it out of one of the numerous attic nooks of the old house last night when he mentioned a baby. He made a note to ask her about it once their guests were settled.

"Well, maybe Martin babies have been using high-class furniture, but Harper babies definitely use dresser drawers for a couple of months. Then when they get too big for the drawer, we go looking for a secondhand crib.'' Lori said it without any sign of pain or regret.

"It's really very practical that way.'' She smoothed the blanket, and settled the drawer next to the bed. "I mean, bassinets and cradles are pretty useless pieces of furniture unless you have a huge house. And we've never had a house, let alone a huge one to store anything in.''

He must have shown the pang of guilt he felt, because Lori crossed the distance between them quickly. "Hey, I didn't mean to offend you or anything. That's just the way life is. I mean, we're still better off than the Birthday Boy, aren't we?''

"Huh?" Okay, so it wasn't eloquent. He was too short on sleep to be anything but dense.

"Jesus, silly. He didn't have a house to be born into. The best His folks could do was a stable and a feeding trough in a strange city. And things turned out okay after that. I figure in comparison, we're doing great."

Then why was her lip trembling? Mike followed his instincts and put his arm around her. "Hey, it's going to be okay."

She leaned against him and he was overpowered by the scent of her. It was warm and clean and comforting all at the same time and he fought the urge to bury his face in her hair, lift her off her feet and envelop her.

Instead, he just leaned his forehead down to touch the top of her head. She felt so slight in his arms, and her shoulders trembled for a moment. "I know. I know. But sometimes it's just so hard."

"Being both mommy and daddy to Tyler, and now the baby, too?"

"Mostly that, I guess. The hardest part is knowing I don't have to be both all the time. That God really is in charge and looking out for all of us every minute of every day. That, Mike, is the hardest part. I feel better when I'm holding the reins."

"Well, sure. Don't we all." His arm tightened around her instinctively.

"Yes, but see, it doesn't have to be that way. That's the beauty of really knowing Jesus. You can let go of the worries and the wondering. At least that's how it's supposed to work. If you're good enough at it, I'm pretty sure that's how it works."

"But you don't know for certain?" Mike used his finger to tip her heart-shaped face up to him. She felt so wonderful. Could he kiss away the pain that he saw there? No, this wasn't the time. He let go of her face.

Her eyes glowed with unshed tears. "No. Not for certain. Because I'm never good enough."

"Lady, if you're not good enough, then I definitely don't want to know that God you talk about so much. Because if somebody like you doesn't measure up, nobody will."

Lori's head sank, and her eyes closed. "Then I must not be good enough even at explaining all this, because that isn't what I meant. I think I'm just too tired to have this conversation, okay?"

He had to get out of here. If he didn't, soon he was going to be picking her up and tucking her into the frilly white sheets on Gloria's guest bed. The urge to take care of this young woman was way beyond his control. "Fine." He looked around the room. "Is there anything else you need?"

"Just the things out of the bags Carrie brought

back. And Tyler, of course, if your mom will let go of him.''

"I can probably persuade her. They must have read every old picture book in the house by now.''

"Then send him back here, and I'll see you in the morning. I still think we should be setting up housekeeping next door instead of here.'' How could anybody look that determined and that girlish at the same time?

"No way. Not until you're a few days farther from birthing that baby. And we have a phone installed in that place. And I make sure all the doors and windows lock, that there's food in the fridge…''

"Okay, I get your drift. Go get Tyler before you upset your halo.''

"What on earth are you talking about?''

Lori blushed; he was sure of it. It was appealing and attractive. "Nothing. Nothing that makes sense, anyway. Just let me get everybody settled and get some sleep. I promise I'll make more sense in the morning.''

That was almost a shame. This slightly goofy, vulnerable side to Lori was very attractive. Once she had her wits about her in a day or two, it was likely to disappear. And Mike knew he'd miss it when it was gone.

* * *

This bed was almost too comfortable. Lori knew she ought to get up. It was daylight and both children were still asleep in her room. Both children. That thought still took some getting used to.

Tyler slept in a sleeping bag on the plush carpet. He had one arm flung out in classic little-boy fashion and the rest of him wound up in the sleeping bag. Mikayla looked like an angel baby in her makeshift crib. And soon she would be big enough that she'd sound like one, but not yet. All that sighing and squeaking kept Lori awake a good deal of the night.

Now it was morning and she should take advantage of both of them sleeping to grab a shower if she could. Heaven knew when she'd get this opportunity again.

The hot shower was bliss. Lori decided it was the first miracle of the day. Why not hot water as a miracle? Definitely the source of the water, being in the Martins' house and taken care of in this luxury, was a miracle.

Mikayla didn't wake up while Lori dried off and got dressed. That had to count as at least half a miracle. Sweats and leggings still made up most of Lori's wardrobe that fit. Her prepregnancy jeans looked impossibly slender. She sighed and folded them back up, sliding them into the bottom of a bag. So every miracle didn't happen on her time-table. The thought actually made her smile.

Now what? Breakfast and some brainstorming about how to get a phone installed next door on her limited credit. She agreed with all of Mike's conditions for her to move in there. They needed working utilities, a phone and a full refrigerator. She needed to retrieve her car from out at the trailer, and look over things one last time to see if she'd missed anything someone had stolen or tried to find. It was a mystery to her what anybody wanted out there, but obviously somebody knew something she didn't.

She left the door to her room open and went to the kitchen. It was a good thing she'd showered and done her hair, because Mike was already at the table drinking a cup of coffee. And he was the kind of person who woke up clear-headed and good-looking.

Of course he went to bed good-looking, Lori thought, making it an easier process. How had she been this close to him for several days without no-ticing how handsome he was? Maybe because she was busy seeing the good heart inside him. That good heart was packaged in nice wrapping, she had to admit. Mike looked freshly showered, too; dark hair slicked back and face shaved to show off that cute cleft in his chin.

"Good morning." Lori should have been expecting him to speak. But why did it make her jump?

"Hey. Happy Boxing Day."

"Sure. Want to go a few rounds?"

Lori giggled. "Not that kind of boxing, silly. Don't you have any class? It's a British thing. The day after Christmas you go visit the relatives and bring goodies..."

"And boxes?"

"One would assume. It's one of the many strange holidays I know about."

"Is there a girl manual you people are issued that gives you instructions about those things? I swear my mother knows all that stuff, too."

"No manual. But I used to love parties when I was a kid, could never get enough of them. So I found every excuse I could to make one."

"Good. We need more parties around here."

"Oh?" Lori found a coffee cup set out next to the pot, and poured herself a cup. Maybe she should have waited to be served, but this morning she needed the real stuff. "I would have thought your mom would be a party expert."

"She is, but hers tend to be on the gala side. I like backyard barbecues and Monopoly marathons better."

Lori nodded. "Sounds like more my speed. Did we keep you up any last night?"

"Not a bit. My apartment is too far from where you are to hear much. How about you? Is my namesake the model baby?"

Lori looked around, wondering how to ask about breakfast. "She is, to tell the truth. I mean, she didn't sleep through the whole night, but people who are two days old seldom do. She got up twice, ate and went back to sleep."

"Good." Mike got up from the kitchen table. "I'm forgetting my manners. Mom will shoot me when she gets up. Can I get you some breakfast? I don't eat much myself in the morning, just toast or cereal or something. You're probably starved."

"I could eat," Lori admitted. "But I don't want you to go to any trouble. Cereal would be fine."

He led her to a walk-in pantry. Lori kept herself from going goggle-eyed. It was the size of her kitchen. There were appliances she couldn't identify, and enough boxes and cans to stock a small grocery. "Wow. Your mom really likes to cook."

Mike laughed. "That she does. Now, when she has those parties, the gala ones, somebody else caters. But for us, cooking is her relaxation."

"Sounds like you reap the benefits of her relaxing."

"We work things out. I do most of the outside

stuff around the place, the yard anyway. We lease out the farm land mostly, when she doesn't run her goofy goats.''

Lori picked a box of cereal off one of the shelves. ''She sounds like a woman of many talents.''

''I guess. Between you and me, the goats are more of a pain than an asset. But they are as friendly as dogs around her. I'm surprised she didn't have Tyler out seeing them yesterday.''

''I think she did. Now I understand his comments about feeding the funny-looking dogs while we were gone.'' Lori giggled. ''I guess they were funny looking, for dogs.''

Mike had a nice smile. She could get used to seeing him this cheerful. ''They bark funny, too. The real dog just goes nuts trying to figure them out. Now let's get you fed before you starve.''

Lori waved him off. ''I'm okay, really.''

''Sure. But how long do you think we're going to have this house to ourselves this way? You know we'll have a kid or two up soon, and Mom with them.''

''True. Just about the time I pour milk on this stuff most likely. You get used to it after a while.'' Of course Lori was still getting used to having two children depend on her, but she wasn't about to let Mike know how vulnerable she felt. If he saw her as a competent, together person and mother, that was great.

She got more than halfway through her cereal before Tyler bounded into the room. "Can we watch cartoons? Is it Saturday?"

"And good morning to you. How did you sleep?"

"Great. But 'Kayla squeaks."

"Uh-oh. Is she squeaking now?"

He shook his head and Lori eased back into her chair. "Not now. But she sure did last night, didn't she? Is she gonna do that all the time?"

"For a while. But soon you'll be back in your own room and you won't hear her as much. Will that be better?"

"A lot." Tyler pushed his shock of blond hair out of his face and looked relieved. "Can I watch cartoons now?"

"It's not Saturday. Mike has box cereal every morning for breakfast." Lori looked at her confused breakfast companion. "See, at our house sugared cereal in a box is a Saturday-morning treat. The rest of the time it's toast or oatmeal or something more nutritious." And cheaper, she could have added in honesty.

She turned back to Tyler, who was wide-eyed and grinning. "Box cereal every morning? This is cool."

"Yeah, well, don't get too used to it. When life goes back to normal, you'll get this sugary stuff only on Saturday morning."

"Then I hope we stay here a while. I like cereal every morning!" Tyler got up on a chair, sharing a grin with Mike.

"And I like having company. How long do you think we can talk your mom into doing this?" Looking between the two of them, Lori wasn't sure who was having a better time. She grinned. Two and a half miracles already and breakfast wasn't over. It was starting to be a pretty good day.

Chapter Eight

"**Y**ou sure you're up to this?" Mike cast a worried glance Lori's way across the car seat.

Lori thought he looked less comfortable driving his mother's car than his own truck. It touched her that he was willing to go through some discomfort just to have Mikayla's car seat fit better here than in the truck. Another example of his care and concern for them. "If I weren't, I'd tell you. Rest assured of that."

"Okay. I guess I'm not used to new babies or new moms. I mean, I'm still surprised you're up and around already."

"Believe me, women have been doing this for centuries. And most of us get right up and do stuff. And you said if I was good for a week we could get moving." Lori looked out the window. The winter scenery didn't offer much to make conversation about. "I still think it's a little silly telling the sheriff about all this."

"Well, I don't. And Carrie doesn't. So we're going to tell him. We don't have to go through all the details of filing an official report unless you find something missing later. But Hank ought to know."

"All right." Agreeing was easier than arguing with him. "Then afterward we'll stop and get the things I need from the store and go home."

"Where everybody will take a nap."

"Not me. I don't take naps!" Tyler protested loudly from the back seat.

"I know that. I should have said everybody who needs one will take a nap."

"Okay. While they're taking a nap, can I help Miss Gloria with the goats?"

Tyler and the goats were old buddies by now. Lori wondered how much Mike's mother was altering her normal routine so that she and the little boy could visit with the goats every afternoon. She was grateful to her for the time she spent with her active son.

"Looks like we got lucky," Mike said, rousing Lori out of her thoughts. "We're not even going to have to go to Hank's office to make that statement.'' He pulled the car into a space in front of the Town Hall Restaurant.

Lori had never been inside the local landmark. She was probably the only person within fifty miles of Friedens that hadn't been there for at least one cup of coffee. ''How can you tell Hank is here?''

''His car's parked out front. And he never leaves it anyplace he can't see it'' was Mike's succinct reply.

It took a moment to get everybody out of the car, including Mikayla in the car seat, and to caution Tyler that even though they were going into the restaurant, it did not mean he was having ice cream at ten in the morning.

The bell over the door clanged when Mike pushed the door open, motioning them through. Lori walked in to the welcome warmth of the place. There in the first booth was a man in uniform who had to be Hank. He looked just as she expected him to.

The sheriff could have been someone's grandfather. He probably was for all she knew. A burly man in uniform with silvering hair, he had a face she could only describe as kind. That was a comfort. It was his companion across the booth that gave her a start.

The other man looked up from their conversation. ''Well, I'll be. Here I sit talking about the little lady and in she walks to the Town Hall.'' Gary's boss stood up. ''That is you, isn't it, Mrs. Harper? And you did go and have that baby. I was telling Hank I thought we needed to put out a search party or something.''

Lori smiled weakly. ''No search party needed, Mr. Hughes. I didn't even know you were looking for me. I guess I didn't think to let you know what was going on.''

Hughes gave the sheriff one of those telegraphed looks that seemed to say *''Women. Do you believe this?''* and Lori's blood pressure rose. Everyone else always thought this man was so wonderful. Why did he set off her alarm bells all the time?

He motioned one well-manicured hand toward the next table. ''We can't leave you standing up. Why don't you and your…friend take a seat?'' His lifted eyebrows begged an introduction to Mike.

The sheriff spoke up before Lori had a chance. ''You don't know Mike Martin? Runs Martin Properties with his mother, and is one of our best fire-and-rescue volunteers. How's that dog of yours, Mike?''

Mike leaned across the table to shake Hank's hand, and made his hellos to Hughes, as well. ''Just fine, Hank. And we've met, but not so Mr. Hughes would probably remember me. What's your connection with Lori?''

His stern expression made Lori feel like he was grilling the other man. Or maybe she was the one on the spot. She hadn't thought to tell Mike about Gary's boss and his ownership of the trailer they were renting. Before Hughes could answer, something dawned on her.

"Mr. Hughes owns the trailer we rent, Mike. And he may have been checking up on us. This whole trip into town might be a waste of time after all."

"It's your place?" Mike's normally friendly brown eyes were narrow. He didn't seem to have much more use for Hughes than Lori did.

"Sure. Not much else out there on that patch of land I got from my uncle. He left me the place when he passed on a couple of years ago." Hughes smiled and Lori was reminded of something reptilian. Why didn't anybody else see the man that way?

"So you rented it to the Harpers?"

"When Gary came to work for me. You did know he was working delivery for me at the feed store, didn't you? When he had his, uh, accident I thought the least I could do was let Lori and the little boy stay for six months, rent free."

"And give them a car." *If you could call it that,* Mike's unspoken words finished the sentence.

This was almost too much. Lori didn't trust the

man who had employed her husband. But he was a good Christian, a successful business owner and everybody else in Friedens seemed to think the world of him. "It was very kind of Mr. Hughes to do everything for us that he did. Somehow I never thought about him looking for us when Carrie asked who might have a key to the place."

"Why don't we all sit down, and explain this to me before my coffee gets cold," Hank said. "I see at least one fella who could probably use a dough-nut."

Tyler bounced from one foot to the other. "Can I? I'm hungry again, Mom."

"What a surprise. Yes, Tyler, let's get you some-thing to eat and I'll find a pencil so you can draw on the place mat." Between the two things, he could stay quiet for the few minutes they would need to talk to Hank and Mr. Hughes.

They settled in at the table, Mikayla's seat taking up a large portion of it. The efficient waitress cooed over the baby and got Mike's coffee and glasses of milk for Lori and Tyler. Once she was done serving them, Hank leaned over toward their table.

"Now, why don't you explain all this to me. Mike, you seem to have tracked me down on pur-pose. What for?"

Lori could barely look Mike in the face. He seemed unhappy to be explaining all this, and it was her fault that he was on the spot. "Lori's been staying out at our place. We went by Christmas Day to pick up some things for her and the kids, out to the place she's renting from you," he said, motioning to Hughes. "Somebody had been there since she had the baby."

"Anything missing?"

"No, that was the odd part. Plenty of stuff disturbed, but nothing gone. Still, I told her that we needed to report the disturbance, in case something else happened."

"And you're right. Did whoever went through the place break in, Mrs. Harper?"

Lori shook her head. She felt so silly now. "No. And when Mike and Carrie asked about who else had a key, it didn't dawn on me that Mr. Hughes might have come out to check on us and tried to find out where we were."

Hughes smiled. It was still not a smile that she trusted. "And that's what happened. But we still have a little problem, because I didn't touch much of anything. I was concerned that nobody was there, and it looked like you folks had left in a hurry. But aside from opening a drawer or two looking for an address book or something that might tell me where you went, I certainly didn't disturb anything. It's not my right, even as a land-lord, to just root through things."

How did he know things had been rooted through unless he did it? Lori's head snapped up and she looked at Hughes. His bland expression challenged her. What was she thinking? How could she accuse him of anything, when he was the trusted wealthy man who'd lived here for a lifetime and she was at the receiving end of his charity? She looked down at the table again.

Mike had caught the change in her expression and seemed to be asking her something silently. She refused to look straight at him. There was nothing she could do about this situation of her own making. Better to just keep quiet.

"I don't know what else to say," she finally said quietly. "Nothing was taken, and I didn't think about Mr. Hughes having a key, or looking for us when we were gone. I guess I wasted everybody's time."

Hughes laughed. His chuckle set her teeth on edge with its oily smoothness. "I don't consider my time wasted. I was just telling Hank that my tenants were missing and I was concerned. I didn't know whether to start calling hospitals looking for you. Now that you've shown up here, I don't have to worry."

He stood up, and the other men stood with him. Lori reached out a hand to Mikayla's infant seat to give her a reason to stay sitting. The baby was stirring, but not fully awake. "Well, I'm glad the trip was worth something. And we won't be bothering you again."

"Definitely. Lori and Tyler and the baby are moving in with us. It's been very decent of you to let them have your place for this long, but I'm sure you understand. Do we need to settle anything up?" Mike looked at Hughes with a challenge that made Lori flush.

Who was this man? Why did he think her welfare was his concern? If she had other options she would walk out of the diner right now and prove to him she was capable of supporting her family just fine, without his constant help. But she wasn't. Her options besides staying at the Martins' were few and unpalatable. So Lori closed her mouth on the angry words she was tempted to let fly.

"No settling needed." Hughes waved a hand. "Let me know when they're officially moved out. If you'd come by the feed store and turn in the keys, Mrs. Harper, I'd be obliged."

"Certainly. As soon as I make sure everything's out of there." Lori hadn't intended on that being very soon, but now she was determined that another week would not pass without seeing Hughes and giving him back his key. The sooner she could owe the man nothing, the better.

Of course she would still have the Martins that

she owed plenty to. But at least she could work for Gloria. And unlike Hughes, she trusted both of them. It was a better situation, even though she wasn't totally comfortable.

"Well, I'll let you all get on with your breakfast," Hughes said. "Thanks for listening to me, Hank. Glad I wasn't any trouble after all."

"You never are, Clyde." The sheriff waved away the other man's thanks. "I'll catch up to you later."

Hughes went to the cash register, exchanged pleasantries while he paid his bill and left. "Well, I'm glad you showed up," Hank said. "There was something about that whole situation that struck me as odd. Meaning no offense, Mrs. Harper—"

"Lori, please," she interjected.

"Lori, then…but Clyde Hughes usually isn't that concerned about anybody. You sure nothing is missing in that place?"

"Pretty sure." Did this mean the sheriff didn't like Hughes any more than she did? "There just wasn't much worth taking. I'm not proud of saying it, but we were living pretty close to the bone."

Hank nodded. "I got that impression. Mr. Hughes comes off as being the generous soul for letting you have the place rent free, but if I remember correctly, it wasn't much better than a fish camp. Definitely no place I'd put a family to live."

The sheriff paused for a moment. He seemed to be thinking while he drank his coffee. Setting down the cup, he went on. "If you'll pardon me for bringing up something painful, I still have more questions than answers about the way your husband died. Since he was working for Hughes at the time, and driving his vehicle, it makes me a little curious."

Lori cleared her throat. "I wanted to ask you something about that. At the hospital I overheard something that makes me think there was suspicion that Gary was dealing drugs. Then when we were going through my things after the break-in, we came across Gary's death certificate. When they came to tell me, the officers said he drowned when his car ran off the road. It seemed simple."

"Nothing ever is, though." Hank stopped talking while the waitress refreshed his coffee and Mike's. "Thanks, Katy." When she moved on to the next table, he began again. "The medical examiner said the primary cause of death was drowning, but he had a lot of reservations. The tox screen he ran was kind of strange, and it looked like somebody could have helped your husband off the road."

"Why didn't anybody tell her this before?" Mike broke in before Lori could ask.

"None of it would have brought the man back," Hank said bluntly, looking more stern than grandfatherly. "And the less anybody knew, the less whoever had a hand in this would be suspicious."

"And you couldn't rule out the fact that I might have had a hand in it myself," Lori said quietly.

"There was that, at first. Once I'd met you, and my investigator had, that wasn't a concern. But yes, it's always a factor," Hank admitted. "Most people are killed by someone they know well."

Killed. The word dropped like a rock into the charged atmosphere between them. "Are you sure about this?"

"No. That's the other reason that I didn't say anything to you. No offense, ma'am, but I don't have any firm proof that whatever your husband took that made him go off the road wasn't self-administered. Or that he knew all about the things we found in that trunk."

"I understand. But I told you then, and I'll say it now, that whatever Gary's other faults, I never knew him to use drugs or drink." He always said that was for other suckers, Lori added silently. Besides, he didn't have the money.

"I know. And you would probably know best."

"Which means you're left with a lot of unanswered questions, including who besides Hughes tossed that trailer," Mike said. "Makes me glad to be out of the loop."

"I'll take you as part of my loop anyday, Mike.

Just say the word and your mother will be out a vice president in that company of hers.''

Mike's smile seemed weak. ''Thanks for the offer, Hank. But I've said it before and I'll say it now. I really like the property-management business.''

''Which is why you spend more time volunteering for fire-and-rescue than you do at a desk.'' Hank's eyes twinkled, but his face was solemn. Lori could tell it wasn't the first time the men had sparred verbally on this subject.

She felt uncomfortable being in the middle of the discussion. When Tyler upset his milk a moment later it was a welcome distraction. She could have hugged him for providing the diversion. And of course, by the time the milk had been cleaned up, Mikayla was awake and any calm time for discussion was over.

Lori hurried out of the diner. ''These kids came in handy,'' Mike said softly as they left. ''They got me out of a bind in there. Hank just will not believe that I would rather write up property contracts and deeds than look for missing people with Dogg.''

''I'm glad you're grateful for the disturbance,'' Lori said, jiggling the infant seat on the way to the car. ''But why do I have as hard a time believing the part about property deeds as Hank seems to?''

His expression said Mike didn't have a good answer. He unlocked the car and motioned her in silently, and Lori busied herself looking after her daughter instead of grilling him.

Chapter Nine

Lori was a human dynamo. What she accomplished in a short amount of time continued to surprise Mike. When she cleared out the trailer in less time than he thought one human could, and settled in at his mom's house in fewer than ten days, he marveled at her stamina.

"So, are you satisfied now?" Mike asked as they walked out of the feed store into crisp January air. "I thought you were going to drive me nuts until we gave that man back his keys."

"I'm satisfied." Lori's voice was firm and her eyes sparkled. It reminded him again that she was a very attractive woman. "At least with that part. I hate owing people. Which is why I'm not satisfied with my current situation, Michael."

"Oh, don't call me that." He grimaced. "Mike, please. Michael is what my mom uses when she's unusually peeved at me. Which she will be if she thinks I've been letting you do too much already."

"Not her problem." Lori shrugged. She was one incredibly stubborn woman. "I still owe you and your mother far too much that you haven't let me start paying back. Mikayla's over three weeks old. The doctor has released me to drive and do anything I like. Why can't I start that cleaning that you promised me?"

Hopeless. Arguing with Lori was becoming a daily event and Mike never felt like he won. "Anything else you're good at that might be less taxing? Ever done data entry or other computer work? There's always a raft of paperwork to catch up with at the office."

"Which I'm sure you just love doing yourself." She had him on that one. "As a matter of fact, I used to be pretty good at that kind of stuff. I'm sure the programs have changed since I've had a chance to learn them. Two or three years out of work in that business is like an eternity."

"But you could catch up quickly. You're a fast learner."

Lori stopped on the sidewalk with a bemused smile that made her look tempting. She really needed a kiss on the nose, somehow. Mike put away the thought. "Thank you. I appreciate the compliment. But how did you figure that out about me?"

"Lots of things." Where did he begin? With the fact that in less than a month she knew where everything in the house was, and what his mother would and wouldn't get upset about Lori doing during the day while she and Mike were at work.

Or how about the way she'd adapted to the needs of two active kids when she had only had one weeks before? Perhaps the biggest one was that it had only taken her two or three tries to figure out that Mike wasn't interested in talking about Jesus with her, no matter how often she brought the subject up. Now if he pointed that one out, he would only be Michael again so he took that answer out of the lineup.

"Hey, you're resourceful," he said, getting into the truck and unlocking her side door. "I mean, I've only seen you bring two little bags of clothes to the house, but I don't think I've ever seen you wear the same thing twice in one month."

She looked away, but Mike could see a dimple on her left cheek deepen the way it did when she grinned. Another definitely kissable spot. "I didn't think you would notice something like that. Most guys don't."

How could they fail to notice when presented

with such an attractive package daily? Mike didn't say that, knowing it would only get him in trouble. "Then I pity them. But seriously, I think we could use the office help a lot more than the heavy cleaning."

"Let's talk to your mom when we get home. If she feels the same way, then I could start going down there half days soon. I could get a lot done with Mikayla sleeping. She still takes more naps than she stays awake. And maybe we could get Tyler into morning preschool."

She planned ahead. Mike wondered if she had been considering this before today. It was more than likely. The weeks that Lori had lived at the house, slowly moving more of her things next door all the time, had been a learning experience for him.

When she first came to them, all Mike saw was a fragile new mother alone. The desire to protect her and take care of her was overwhelming. But she didn't let him give in to that desire. Slowly but surely, in a thousand small ways, Lori Harper had shown him that she was willing and able to look out for her little family and herself. Her financial resources might be small, but her determination was giant-size.

It was almost as large as the respect he'd grown to have for her. Or maybe the attraction, as well.

No sense admitting either. He'd be Michael again for certain. Better just head the truck out to the house and talk to Mom about the office work. Maybe that would get his mind off the bounce in Lori's step in slim blue jeans as she walked out of Hughes's feed store, obviously feeling like a free woman.

Lori didn't think they'd been gone long. Certainly no more than an hour, at most. Still, a welcoming committee marked their return to the Martin house as if they'd been to the North Pole and back.

Tyler was waiting at the door. "Good, Mom. You're home. 'Kayla cried so hard, she threw up. Miss Gloria can't make her happy."

Lori hurried through the kitchen and into the family room where she could hear her daughter wailing and Gloria pacing, even on the carpet. "Hush now. It's all right. Mama will be back soon." Gloria sounded near tears.

"Mom's back. Tyler says she 'threw up.' I hope it wasn't anything major."

Gloria gave her a look of sheer relief as she handed over the howling infant. Were her hands shaking? It didn't fit the picture of the calm, confident woman Lori had seen over the last few weeks. "There certainly seemed to be a lot of it. I don't think I was holding the bottle right. And she didn't seem to like taking one, anyway.''

''Nursing babies don't always like somebody else trying to feed them.'' Lori put her unhappy daughter on her chest; the baby's arching neck supported and her head looking over Lori's shoulder while she firmly patted her back. ''Right now I think she's just more mad than anything.'' As she talked, the baby's crying subsided into more of a grumbling than anything, her mouth pressing against Lori's shoulder and her own clenched fist.

''Good. I was afraid I'd done something wrong and she was sick.'' Gloria sat down on the sofa, looking like she'd been through a train wreck. Lori surveyed the room. Signs of the struggle were everywhere. A receiving blanket lay draped over a chair, Tyler's toys were strung about where they'd obviously been picked up in efforts to distract the baby, and tossed down when they didn't work.

The bottle was on the rug near the heavy oak-and-leather Mission rocker, and Gloria's pumps weren't far from it. That this together lady had kicked off her shoes worried Lori as much as anything. She wasn't the type to appear less than perfectly attired in front of people, even in her own home. ''She's not sick. You, however, look like you need a vacation.''

Gloria smiled weakly. ''I don't think little babies

are my strong point. They never have been. I just don't have the background.''

''I know. I felt that way the first time around with Tyler. I'd been an only child myself, and my family moved around so much, nobody hired me as a baby-sitter. I was always the new girl in town. Did you have any family nearby when Mike was a baby?''

''Not really. That was different,'' Gloria said. ''He was already...'' She trailed off and shook her head, passing a hand over her eyes. ''Already the perfect baby by the time he was this age,'' she finished.

It wasn't what Lori felt Gloria had planned to say. There was a suspicion growing in her that she couldn't voice yet. If she had to finish that sentence the way she thought Gloria planned to, she would have said Mike was already out of this stage when he came to Gloria.

So many little things pointed to Mrs. Martin not being comfortable or even familiar with babies, even though she was Mike's mother. If what Lori suspected was true, it was one of the best-kept secrets she'd ever seen. And if that was the case, Gloria had her reasons. It wasn't Lori's job to try and find out what those reasons were. Nor was it any of her business.

Right now she had a very evident and pressing

job. Walking over to the spot on the rug where Mikayla's blanket lay, she picked it up and settled her and her daughter into the rocker. Draping the blanket like a private tent over the baby made her frantic stirring slow, then stop. "That's right, lunch is served," she told her daughter softly. "Now maybe we can all get some peace around here." Gloria, at least, looked like she could use several hours of peace.

Lori wasn't sure that Gloria got peace, exactly. What she did get was relaxation in her own way. After a quick lunch she rounded up Tyler and went out to play with the goats. Lori was amused at the difference in the frazzled businesswoman once she put on her jeans and boots and headed out with Tyler right behind. Once they came in from their goat feeding-and-grooming trip, Mike's mother looked more approachable again.

"You look better. More in your element."

Gloria gave her a wry grin in return. "I guess I know about goats than little babies. At least I have more daily contact with them these days. Sorry I was such a pill earlier."

Lori waved off her concern. "Don't worry about it. Taking care of somebody else's new baby isn't easy. Taking care of your own is no picnic, but at least you finally get to the point where you know what they're trying to tell you. It's a lot easier with the ones Tyler's age, isn't it?''

Gloria patted her windblown hair into place. "Definitely. I have to be honest and admit I'm more comfortable with the little guy than the baby. She's beautiful, but I feel out of my league with her." Gloria wrinkled her nose. "Oh, no, a sports analogy. I've been hanging around Mike too long."

They both laughed over that. Lori had noticed that he used a lot of sports themes when he was trying to express himself. "Does Martin Properties have ball teams in the summer? If so, I know who the coach is."

Gloria sat down with a bemused look on her face. "They haven't in a couple of years. But that sure would be a great advertising thing, our name on the uniforms and such. And Mike would jump at the chance to play or coach." She gave Lori a speculative look. "Any more good business ideas?"

Here was the opportunity she needed. *Thanks, Lord,* she breathed silently. "Well, to tell the truth, I do. One big idea, and I don't know how you'll take it."

Gloria leaned back in her chair. "Try me. Mike says I'm a hard case to impress, but that's because his ideas are kind of goofy sometimes. Business isn't his strong suit. Something about you reminds me of myself when I was struggling to learn my husband's business, back when it was just the two of us. I want to hear what you have to say."

Lori felt incredibly blessed. Here was her chance to start truly providing for her family. And it had come about because Mikayla spit up on her surrogate grandmother. Yes, the Lord had a real sense of humor. She took a deep breath and started outlining her plan, sketchy as it was, to Gloria.

Now there were two formidable women. Mike walked into the kitchen where Gloria and Lori sat on opposite sides of the table. There were papers spread out between them in several arcs. A couple of his mom's favorite yellow legal pads were thrown in for good measure and the manual to at least one software program. Why did this somehow feel like forces arrayed against him?

They were quite the forces, anyway. Lori talked in an animated fashion, one hand waving while the other held Mikayla up to her shoulder. She was so alive. Mike couldn't imagine how she could face the world the way she did every day, blue eyes sparkling, ready to take on anything. In her circumstances he'd have a hard time getting out of bed.

Tyler sat at the end of the table away from the women, paying them little heed while he drew a complicated picture that seemed to require every marker in the house. He had a smudge of green on his nose.

"This could work. How do you feel about pre-school?" Mike heard his mother ask. Oh, great, Lori had sprung her plan to work in the office. And his mother thought it was a good idea.

"Fine, if there's a good one nearby. Are there any in Friedens near the office that one of the churches runs? I'd love for Tyler to be in a church preschool at least once before kindergarten next year. Living as far out as we were, there wasn't much choice but to stay home with him. Especially when I found out...about Mikayla."

They both looked at the contented baby on her shoulder and smiled. Mike had to admit the squirt was growing on him. He still felt awkward around her, like his hands were the size of catcher's mitts or something, but she was a sweet baby most of the time, and even smiled once in a while now.

"Great," Gloria said. "Then maybe we can start you out next week. Part days, definitely. And if you do this, there won't be any of that cleaning. I can always get somebody to do that."

Lori sighed. "Oh, all right. But I still think I should pitch in around here once in a while. I'm not pulling my weight."

"Says who?" Mike challenged, entering the conversation whether they wanted him to or not.

The same look of amused tolerance seemed to pass over both the women's faces. "Ah, your knight in shining armor," Gloria chimed in. "Michael, did you know this young lady was better on the computer than you are? And you were going to let her scrub floors around here instead?"

How did this get to be about him? Mike felt like backing off. "It just came up today. And I told her to talk to you about it. I mean, you are still the boss around here, as far as business is concerned."

"Not that I wouldn't like to change that. And maybe bringing in another person into the office is just the way to start the process."

Mike felt walls closing in on him somehow. "What do you mean?"

"Maybe with good help, somebody astute in the paperwork area, you'd be more comfortable with the rest of the business. I know it's not what you'd rather be doing. But it's the family business, and we're it as far as family, if you haven't noticed." Her mouth quirked up in one corner. Mike felt a pang of guilt.

He'd never be the businessman his father was. Even at six he had recognized that his dad liked things about the wheeling and dealing of the business world that just bored him silly. Playing in the creek was more exciting. Training his first puppy kept his attention ten times longer than math at school. And those feelings hadn't ever really changed.

"I know, Mom. And maybe you're right." Mike looked at the two of them at the table.

"So you don't mind? I know it's not what we agreed on originally, but I'd really like to try this." Lori stood and shifted Mikayla higher on her shoulder. "I want to do everything I can to help out around here. And to get back on my feet as quickly as possible. I owe you so much."

"No, I don't mind. Not that I believe that you'd turn around and go back to your original plan if I did."

Lori had a beautiful smile. That dimple in her left cheek got impossibly deep when she was happiest, making Mike want to touch that sweet spot. Or kiss it. Whoa, where was that coming from?

"You know me too well already, Mike. You're right, I wouldn't back down. But it is important that you approve. Especially if we're going to be in the office together every day."

Oh, this was going to be a challenge. Not only evenings now with Lori and Tyler sharing the kitchen table, and their lives. But now most of his day would be spent with the attractive young widow on the premises, as well. Mike could tell his answering smile was weak. "It will be great, like

Mom said.'' The funny part was, he believed it. He was a fool for putting himself in this tempting woman's company for that many hours a day, but he couldn't think of anyplace he'd rather be.

Chapter Ten

It had only taken one weekend to get Tyler registered for preschool at Faith Community Church just two blocks from the office. Lori envisioned walking the short distance to have lunch with him once the weather got a little better. Right now she was willing to stay in the warm office and keep Mikayla sheltered in her corner near the radiator. It was a cozy spot for both of them.

Tyler hadn't fussed much this morning at being left at the preschool. Lori was all set for first-day jitters, or even some waterworks, but Tyler surprised her. He was friendly with his teacher, thrilled to see all the art supplies in the room and all the other kids. When he discovered the classroom also had guinea pigs, he could hardly conceal his readiness to get on with his day...without Lori as a distraction.

"I'll be back before one," Lori told him.

Tyler shifted from foot to foot, nearly dancing in impatience. "Okay. Have a good day," he said, giving her a quick hug and taking off with his new friend Jake to meet the class pets.

"That took a long time," she told his new teacher.

Emily was young and pretty, and she laughed. "Be glad he's well-adjusted. Some of them don't let go of their parents for days."

"I guess. It would have been nice to be a little missed," Lori said wistfully. She shifted Mikayla and the heavy infant seat. "At least he'll be glad to see me by the time I get back."

"I hope so." Emily giggled again. It was a nice sound, and Lori felt good leaving Tyler here among the friendly people and the bright classrooms, with cutouts of Noah and all the animals marching around his room and the walls painted a sunny yellow. "But today is painting with chocolate pudding, so don't be surprised if he's not real anxious to go home."

"Great. I get to take second place to pudding," Lori said, trying not to sound dejected. "At least I've got this one to keep me company. Come on, Kayla, let's go to work."

Work. It was a fascinating concept. By the time she got to the office and stood contemplating the door, someone had gotten there ahead of her. The blinds were up, and when she stepped into the office she could hear coffee perking.

"I'm here. Sorry it took me a few minutes, but it is Tyler's first day..." She looked around for familiar faces. Nobody was in the front room to greet her. Lori wasn't sure what she'd been expecting from the offices at Martin Properties. Maybe something grander than she got in the town's small business district. It was pretty much an office like any other. Gloria used her finesse on things at home. Here, things were pretty standard.

Martin Properties took up the ground floor of a brick building that fronted Elm Street, four buildings down from the place where Elm intersected with Main. There was a large store window in front, plastered with several posters advertising church rummage sales and the high school basketball season, parts of the fabric of life in a small town. It made Lori feel at home to walk into the place.

There were no curtains or drapes on the big front window. A bamboo shade was pulled down when no one was there, and whoever came in first raised it. That kept the office out of plain view when the premises weren't occupied. Lori imagined that was to hide the fact that there were three or four relatively new computer terminals in the front office, and not much of an alarm system.

File cabinets took up a large portion of one wall of the office. The cabinets, and the rest of the furniture, were office-standard green metal, with a couple of the desks and chairs being slightly scarred oak. There was a bookshelf over in one corner, where she figured Mike's desk must be. He didn't strike her as the kind who wanted his own office. Michael would want to be out in the mainstream where he could see what was going on.

Lori also suspected that being out in the front office got him more company and distraction. Gloria's office had a door on it, with frosted glass in the panes set in the door. That didn't surprise her, either. Gloria wasn't someone who wanted to be disturbed constantly.

The door was cracked open a bit now, and Lori suspected that Mike and his mom were both back there getting ready for the day. She looked around and spotted her corner near the front. There was a portable crib there, the blue canvas and mesh sides a match for the one that Mike's mom insisted they had to have when the Harpers moved into the little rental house. Trust Gloria to think of the nicer details. Mikayla would be as comfortable here as she was at home.

Lori got Mikayla out of her fluffy snowsuit and

smoothed down her squiff of pale hair. She put her in the crib on her stomach where she could practice her newfound skill of pushing up off the ground with her arms and lifting her head. No attempt lasted very long yet, but she was working on it.

Lori marveled at what an easy baby her daughter was. She didn't fuss unless she was wet or hungry. Even now when she had begun to be awake for longer periods, she was content to chew on a fist and watch the world go by most of the time. That was a definite, ongoing miracle. She shuddered to think what she'd do right now with a colicky baby.

Patting Mikayla on the back, she was rewarded with a gurgle. It made her laugh a little herself as she headed to the office in back. "You two in there?" she called, opening the door a little more.

"Everybody who got in on time," Mike teased. "I had to make my own coffee."

Gloria wrinkled her nose. "Do not listen to him, Lori. He makes his own coffee every morning. And he will continue to make his own coffee. Which you might want to test a bit before drinking yourself, I might add. It tends to be so strong, you barely need a full cup."

Mike huffed in mock indignation. "Thanks, Mom. Take all the wind out of my sails. Tyler all set at Noah's Ark?"

"Definitely. They have guinea pigs and chocolate pudding. He won't notice if I don't come back before dark.''

''Great.'' Mike's smile looked even more attractive than usual this morning. It was different seeing him in twill pants and a shirt and tie instead of the jeans and T-shirts he favored at home. He didn't look quite as comfortable with a tie on, but Lori had to admit he looked sharp.

''Why is it so great if Tyler doesn't want me to come get him?'' Lori put her hands on her hips.

''We might want to keep you here a while. It being your first day and all. Maybe even take the new hire out to lunch,'' Mike said.

''Oh, we're not going to start that. I have a daughter here to keep me company, and a lot of work to learn and then do. No lunches out for a while. Besides, I brought a perfectly good bag lunch from home.''

Mike looked at his mother. ''This woman is a grind. No wonder you hired her.''

Gloria rolled her eyes. ''It's a good thing that somebody is, Michael. Things do have to get done around here. It's almost tax season, and you know what that means as far as paperwork…''

Mike raised his hands. ''Do I hear the baby crying?''

Lori dashed out of Gloria's office. Mikayla was still happy in the crib. ''No. Was that just an attempt to get us off your back?'' she asked Mike as he trailed her.

Mike shrugged. ''Could be. But I do have extremely good hearing.''

Gloria blew out an impatient puff of air that Lori could hear from the outer office. ''That he does. I think it's all the practice of listening for that fire-and-rescue beeper so hard every day.''

Mike didn't say a word. He simply went to the still-perking coffeepot, deftly poured himself a cup before anything could spatter and went to his desk. He might not have been talking, but he did whistle. His cheerful tune seemed to be ''Hot Time in the Old Town Tonight.'' Lori stifled giggles and went to her own desk to get ready for the day.

Her lovely bag lunch didn't look as tempting by the time she was ready to eat it. By noon she might have been ready for a break from the desk, just as a reward for all the work she'd done. Still, she had to stick to her guns. No sense in letting Mike think he'd won on the first day. Besides, she didn't have lunch money to speak of, and if she went out, he'd end up buying anyway. She really didn't need to owe Mike Martin anything else.

Working at the desk felt good. Mikayla was her usual sunny self, letting Lori get through much more of the paperwork than she'd hoped. The nicest thing was that she was much more proficient with the computer in the office than she'd expected. Things might have changed in the years since she had worked with office programs, but they had been logical changes, at least for her.

Telling Mike that when he came back from lunch was a mistake. "You're kidding. That all makes sense to you?" His brow wrinkled in consternation. "Even that new spreadsheet program?"

"Well, that one is a little complicated," Lori admitted. "I've got questions for your mom, or somebody, about it."

Mike looked relieved. "Good. You couldn't get that far ahead of me in one day. Less than one full day. It just wouldn't be right."

"I didn't expect to get ahead of you in anything. That wasn't my goal. The only thing I want to do is get to the point where I know the basics again as well as I did when I worked in an office regularly."

"For being here less than a day, I'd say you're meeting goals fairly well." Mike still looked like a kid watching somebody cruise off on his bike.

"Hey, I'm thrilled. Want to show me what I don't know about the spreadsheet stuff?"

Mike pulled up a rolling chair from the next vacant desk. "If you think I can do that. What's the problem?"

He'd removed his coat when he came in the office after lunch. When he rolled his chair up close to her, Lori could smell the outdoors about him somehow, the cold crisp air of the Missouri winter caught in his dark hair.

With Mike at her shoulder she was reminded of the difference in their height. Even sitting in similar office chairs, he was probably a head taller than she was. And even though it wasn't two in the afternoon yet, he needed a fresh shave.

Or at least, for some people he would have. Lori had to admit she found the slightly rough look of his dark beard appealing. It might have clashed a bit with his tailored shirt and tie, but it looked very masculine. She could imagine the prickle of his chin beneath her fingertips. The thought made her shiver.

"Am I too close?" His eyes showed concern.

"No. Yes. Let's just say I'm not used to this much, uh, male company."

"So don't think of me as male company. Think of me as a computer tutor."

"That will take some doing," Lori muttered. Mike hadn't moved any farther away, and it was all she could do to think, period. The whole situation seemed to amuse him.

"Now, what was it that you wanted to know about this program?" He reached a hand over her desk and clicked the computer mouse, bringing a spreadsheet onto the screen. "Looks okay to me."

"Then we're in more trouble than I thought. I'm stuck on how to plug in functions I know you're going to need on interest figures." Lori could feel her fingers tingle. "Here, let me show you…" She reached for the mouse to highlight the columns she needed. Mike didn't move his hand, so she just put hers on top of his larger one. For somebody who had just come from outside he had warm hands. It startled her for a moment and she lost her train of thought.

"Where was I?" He leaned in even closer to her and she could feel the warmth of him now along most of her back as he studied the screen along with her.

His voice rumbled in her ear. "I think it was your interest. I mean, interest in figures. No, I mean the interest figures. On the spreadsheet." He leaned his forehead down to her shoulder, and Lori's heart skipped a beat. It felt so good to have him there, leaning on her. "Am I making much sense?"

"Not much. But I don't mind." Had she really said that out loud? "I don't think I'm making much sense, either. Maybe I should have gone out for lunch, or just a walk to clear my head."

"Yeah, sitting in one spot too long will do that to a body." His voice was softer and even closer again. "You want to take a quick stroll around the block? I'll sit here and watch in case Squeaky wakes up."

"Squeaky. Oh, that's just special." Lori turned to talk to him. He was so very close. Whatever she was going to say next stilled on her lips, which were mere inches from his face.

How did she get herself into this situation? All she wanted was help with a computer program. Now the program was the farthest thing from her mind. The closest thing to her mind, and her body, was going to get her into plenty of trouble if she didn't move immediately.

Her feet seemed locked to the floor. One good push would move her chair on wheels away from this near embrace where Mike sat behind her, shoulder to shoulder and both their hands still on the mouse. Lori wanted to argue with her traitorous body. She really had to move—now. But it felt much too good to be this close to Mike.

He must have thought so, too, because he was moving even closer. His eyes widened and he dipped his head down until their lips met. It was a slow kiss, tentative and sweet. Lori wasn't sure she had ever felt anything so marvelous in her entire life.

Still, all her senses screamed that this could not continue. They were in an open office with a huge glass window facing the street, and all of Friedens. This was a fluke; a chance kiss brought on by being too close for too long to an incredibly handsome man. Finally she made her body work. Her feet pushed the chair across the floor, away from Mike's warmth. Her hand left its comfortable place on top of his.

"I'm sorry. I don't know what happened there," she said, trying not to stammer.

"I think I do." His smile was slow as molasses and as darkly sweet. "And I wouldn't mind it happening again."

"Well, I think I would. And will you look at the time! I have to go get Tyler from school, so if the offer to sit at my desk still stands..." Lori took a deep breath, amazed at how rattled and silly she sounded, unable to say anything else until she got under control.

The light dimmed in his sparkling brown eyes. "Oh. Sure. I'll take good care of Mikayla. Take your time."

Lori nearly ran to the coat rack for her jacket. It was all she could do to not grab it so quickly that the whole rack tipped over. That was all she needed, for the coat rack to be as unbalanced as she felt right now. She flew out the door, still hearing the bell jingle overhead after the door closed.

Control. She needed much more of it than she

possessed right now, and fast. How could one little kiss stir her up this much?

As she strode down the block, being stirred up wasn't what disturbed Lori the most. She could understand Mike's kiss having that effect on her. He was handsome, and they'd shared space most of their waking hours for the last few weeks. It was probably only natural that their bodies reacted this way once they finally collided.

No, the disturbance wasn't what rattled Lori the most. It was the *rightness* of the whole experience. Here she was a widow of a few months, with two kids to support and a life to build. She didn't have the luxury of leaning on anybody for anything right now, except her Father in heaven. Yet she felt no shock or shame in Mike's kiss. Having their lips meet was disturbing and alluring, but it didn't feel wrong. That, more than anything, was what stunned Lori as she hiked the several blocks to Tyler's preschool.

She reached the front doors of Faith Community Church and her head was still spinning. The cool breeze on her face hadn't done anything to clear her head or dispel the feel of Mike's kiss on her lips. To do that she would probably have to hike to Juneau.

Chapter Eleven

First day at work. First kiss from Mike. Lori wasn't sure which exhausted her the most. Maybe it was the combination of the two that made her want to go to sleep that night when Tyler went to bed at eight.

If it wasn't for Mikayla having one of her bouncy, awake periods, she might have put on her pajamas right away and gone to bed like Tyler. However, somebody had to be the grown-up and stay up and do a few things during the evening, so Lori elected herself.

She didn't feel much like the person in charge tonight. Surely the person in charge wouldn't have agreed to be kissed like that today. Nor should a responsible woman with two children depending on her for everything enjoy such things so much. Or be unable to get them out of her head. Why did that one kiss insist on replaying itself over and over until Lori could see and feel Mike's embrace without closing her eyes or pausing in folding the basket of laundry in front of her.

It wasn't fair. Surely she should be able to enjoy one harmless kiss and then be able to forget it. Surely Michael had done just that. He wasn't sitting next door remembering every detail of that brief moment like she was. No, he was probably doing some of the paperwork he had left at the end of the day, or watching television.

''Just forget he's over there. You can do that,'' she said out loud. Her words echoed in the small living room.

Hearing the truck start outside, Lori changed her estimation of what Mike was doing. Apparently instead of doing any of the things she imagined, including reviewing their encounter, he was answering a fire-and-rescue call with the rest of the volunteers. Lori looked out the window of the front room in time to see the truck, its removable blue light plugged in and flashing to advertise its status, pulling out of the long gravel drive.

Dear Lord, keep him safe. Let him come back to me all right. The prayer was as natural and easy as any she'd ever prayed. And it dumbfounded her the moment the words were out. Whoever said Michael would come back to *her?* Of course he'd come back safely, as soon as the barn fire or smoldering car, or whatever emergency had called the volunteers, was under control. But he wouldn't be coming back to her. Because he wasn't hers to begin with.

Lori looked down at the laundry she was folding again. Tyler's blue jeans, a soft chambray shirt that she could use for work if she dressed it up with a scarf. Mikayla's little footed sleepers. This was the fabric of her life. Surely there was no room for care and concern for a man. Not even one as attractive and available as Mike Martin.

Except that he had worked his way into her life, becoming part of the fabric as strongly woven in as the laundry in front of her. How had that happened? They'd only known each other a short time. He cared for her, but surely not in any romantic kind of way. He liked the kids. He'd kissed her once. And here she was praying for his safety while she folded laundry in her living room.

"Face it. You're falling in love with him." Lori's words, spoken aloud, echoed off the walls even louder than her earlier statement had. The words were true. And they scared her half to death. What business did she have falling in love? It wasn't the time or the place for such things. Surely it wasn't part of God's plan for her life at this point, was it?

Lori looked out the front window, neatly framed by heavy green drapes. How did she figure that part out? For starters, she didn't need to turn on the radio while she folded the rest of the laundry. She needed to spend the time in prayer instead. Perhaps that would give her a clearer idea of where Mike fit into her life.

Even if it didn't, prayer time was never wasted. Lori smiled and reached back into the laundry basket. "Hey, that's a good thing about the kids being asleep," she said, finding another pair of Tyler's little white socks. "Nobody will look at me funny while I talk to You out loud, Lord." Sometimes you had to grab those miracles, no matter how small, wherever they came.

The crunch of tires on the gravel outside woke Lori much later. She had fallen asleep sitting up in the chair by the window. Shaking her head to clear the cobwebs that felt as if they'd gathered there, she looked out the window. It was Mike and the truck, both looking none the worse for wear. Good. Now maybe she could go to bed and have a peaceful night.

Mikayla was down to waking up only once a night. Lori, walking down the darkened hallway, prayed that this would be the night she slept until five or six in the morning for the first time. That would be a little miracle in itself. How long was it until babies slept all the way through a seven- or eight-hour stretch? She tried to tax her brain into remembering that far back with Tyler.

It was definitely later than the five weeks Mikayla had been around. But not a whole bunch longer, was it? Pushing her hair away from her face, she stretched and padded into the bedroom without turning on a light. Tomorrow she'd see if Tyler's new preschool had a library, with child-development books in it. She felt like she needed a refresher course in Newborn 101.

By the time she dropped Tyler off at school the next morning, Lori was sure one book wasn't going to solve all her parenting problems. Tyler had dawdled through breakfast and insisted on setting up some complicated block contraption to house his fire engine while she dressed Mikayla. She never could find the scarf that would have dressed up the chambray shirt she wore, and she felt stressed and hurried as she pulled the resisting Tyler into preschool.

"I want to go home. I wasn't done building," he still protested.

"The blocks will be there when you get home this afternoon. And they have blocks at school."

Lori tried not to sound as exasperated as she felt. Where was all the joy she usually felt in the morning with the kids? Even Mikayla seemed to sense her grouchy mood today and fussed all the way to Friedens in her car seat.

Now she wanted the blanket off that covered her seat and prevented her from seeing anything inside the church building on the way to Tyler's classroom. Lori dodged her daughter's flailing hands and feet to lift the blanket.

"It's going straight back on when we leave. You don't need a cold." She knew the baby didn't understand a word she was saying, but that had never stopped her before.

Tyler used the opportunity of being let loose in the hallway to jam his hood back on and turn around. "I really, really want to go home and build. And I miss my fire engine," he said.

"Tyler Harper, I am not going to repeat myself. I am also not going to chase you." Lori stood still in the hallway for emphasis. Tyler turned around, knowing he had pushed the limit. "I know you want to go home right now. But Miss Gloria and Mr. Mike are expecting me to go to work so we can get things done. If I don't get my work done this morning, they won't get all theirs done, either."

"And then the goats will be hungry." Tyler

pushed his hood back. Lori marveled at how well he could put together a chain of events. "I guess I better go to school. Sorry, Mom."

She ruffled his hair. "No problem. And I'm sorry if I sounded mad. I'm not mad, just…rushed, I guess."

Tyler's forehead wrinkled. "Me, too. That's a good word. 'Rushed.'" He said it with a whoosh of air that blew his blond bangs away from his face, making Lori laugh.

"We'll have to do something about that, won't we? The rushing?" She made a similar sound to the one Tyler had made, which got him giggling, too. His laughter made Mikayla smile and in an instant her morning was turned around. Funny how simple most solutions were when you let them happen. Tyler opened the classroom door and headed in to the delightful rumpus that was morning at preschool. It made Martin Properties look very calm in comparison.

How did she do it? Mike looked at Lori, working at the computer calmly entering figures, the phone pressed to one ear while her left hand jiggled Mikayla's crib. The woman was amazing. In the short time she'd been at work in the office she'd found so many ways to fit in.

He had been worried about her managing the

baby and learning the operations around here. For Lori it hadn't seemed to be a problem. She picked up on Gloria's way of doing things quickly, and they communicated better than he'd ever seen his mother get along with any of the part-timers in the office.

Her awful old car kept chugging along between the little green house and town every morning and afternoon and she was never late. A lot of evenings she declined Gloria's invitation to share dinner with them, although Mike did notice that she took her up on using the washer and dryer at the "big house" any time his mom offered.

Mike's own phone ringing pulled him away from his careful observation of Lori. That was a shame, because when she got really involved in what she was doing with the computer, or jiggling the baby, she had this habit of running the tip of her tongue over her pink lips while she concentrated. That he could definitely watch for quite some time.

"Martin Properties."

"And even Martin speaking." Hank's voice was jovial. "Haven't seen you around much lately. Which is a good thing, I guess, because it means there hasn't been much search work around here."

"That's true. But I don't expect a busy man like you called here just to ask why I haven't been over to the station lately."

"You got me there. I need to speak to the lovely lady on your end of the phone. Is she available?"

"Lori's talking to a client right now. Can I have her call you?" Mike wondered what the sheriff wanted with Lori. Surely their business together was wrapped up.

The other man's chuckle was dry and slow. "What if I was to tell you I wanted to talk to your mother? There *is* more than one lovely lady working for Martin Properties these days. Although I'm sure you have eyes for them both differently than I do."

Hank wanted to talk to his mother and was calling her a lovely lady? Surely this had to be chamber of commerce business or something. Mike couldn't imagine another reason for Hank to want to talk to his mother. "Sure. I'll check and see if she's free."

Gloria sounded happy to talk to Hank on the phone. And judging from her enthusiasm in picking up the call, maybe it wasn't chamber of commerce business after all. Mike decided he was going to have to give Hank another good look. Sure, he was widowed and about sixty. And Gloria was, when you got down to it, the most attractive single woman in Friedens of a certain age.

But surely his mother wasn't interested in lunch with Hank Collins for anything but business, was she? Mike breathed a sigh of relief when she came out of the office asking Lori to go to lunch with them at the Town Hall. Lunch for three sounded much more likely to be business.

Still, the whole thing had him a little confused. If it was all business, why did his mother dash back into her office and come out smelling of cologne, with freshly applied lipstick? And why were she and Lori giggling as they left the office with Mikayla packed in her infant seat?

Mike considered closing up for half an hour and just happening to take lunch at the Town Hall today. But since he only did that once in a blue moon it would be obvious what he was up to. Checking up on the lovely ladies he worked with, and why either of them wanted to have lunch with the sheriff. And although he was dying to know the answers, Mike wasn't a snoop. So he manned the phones and finished the proposal he was working on for a strip mall just off the highway. But that girlish giggling from Lori and his mother as they left taunted him the entire time they were gone.

At first Lori thought she was just a chaperon at the Town Hall. Why else would the sheriff and Gloria Martin want her around, complete with the baby, in the middle of a crowded lunch rush? With the presence of the two of them, not even the worst busybodies in Friedens could assume that their meeting was a date of any kind.

Lori wasn't sure why Hank and Gloria had to be that careful anyway. If they wanted to see each other socially, what would stop them? They had both been alone for years; Gloria, she knew, for decades. And although Mike didn't notice it, his mother was still young at heart and an active woman who probably missed having male companionship.

Still, he would have blown a gasket at the thought of his mother going out on a date with the sheriff. Lori could have predicted that, so she ordered her chicken salad on toast, with a glass of milk to go with it and sat back to rock Mikayla in her seat and pretend she wasn't listening to the conversation at the table.

It surprised her when after the small talk was made for a few minutes, Hank turned to her. "I guess you know why you're in on this." Lori nearly choked on the milk she was drinking.

"Well, I thought I did," she said once she recovered. "I just figured I was the, uh, cover here. Sort of like a chaperon, not that you two need one or anything but…"

Hank and Gloria were both laughing. Lori thought Gloria looked great this way, away from the office and smiling in the company of a handsome man. She ought to do it more often. The skin around Hank's eyes crinkled when he laughed, making him seem years younger than he usually did, sitting somber in his uniform. He shook his head, denying her statement. But Lori noticed that even as he denied it, one hand slipped softly over Gloria's.

"You young people have one-track minds, I swear." The sheriff still sounded tickled. "If I wanted to date Mike's mom, I'd do it in less public places than the Town Hall. Even with a chaperon. There are restaurants in Washington, you know, and it's only twelve miles away. No, we're getting you away from the office this time. You see, Ms. Harper, I've got a little proposition for you."

"A proposition that would make my son even more aggravated than the thought of my dating Hank," Gloria said, still smiling. She hadn't moved her hand out from under the sheriff's larger one, Lori noticed. She wasn't sure which was more interesting—the two of them holding hands, or the unspecified proposition that they were talking about.

The waitress came with their lunch, and the sheriff and Gloria stopped holding hands. When the waitress was gone with her tray, Lori took a couple of bites of her chicken salad sandwich, wondering how long she should delay asking them what they had in mind. She didn't want to look too eager.

Her reticence seemed to be bothering Gloria. She picked at her hamburger, rearranging lettuce and tomatoes and thin slivers of red onion. "Aren't you even going to ask?" she finally blurted.

"I suppose so. But I think I've already figured part of it out. The only thing you two have in common that would drive Mike this crazy has to do with Clyde Hughes." It was fun watching the surprise spread over both their faces. "You know I don't trust the man, either, so it must be something to catch him in whatever he's doing. And I've got no doubt he's doing something that isn't quite right."

Hank broke into a grin. "See, Gloria, I told you she was smart."

Gloria's answering grin was even wider. "No, Hank, I told you first. And my son's every bit as smart, so if we're going to do this without him knowing about it, we better be quick. Tell Lori what we had in mind."

Lori leaned over the table, hoping Mikayla wouldn't pick this moment to wake up. Not now when things were getting interesting. She slept like the angel baby she was. And Hank leaned in to the middle of the table, as well.

"You see, it's like this," he began. "Gloria's

right. We're pretty sure ol' Clyde is up to something illegal. Something involving drugs. Probably the meth labs that have been popping up around here. But there's nothing to prove it. Still, when he got so interested in you a few weeks ago, and you living out in his trailer and all that, it got me to thinking."

Hank leaned back, brow furrowed. "I don't know quite how to ask this part. Did your husband know about the baby?" He gestured toward Mikayla's infant seat. "Did he seem worried about having another mouth to feed?"

Lori looked down at the table. Hank was getting very close to an issue she'd dismissed from her own mind several times. "He did seem worried at first. But then he stopped talking about it. And he told me everything was going to be okay."

"Did he say why? Was he getting a raise at work? Taking on another job?" Hank's gaze was piercing. Lori searched her memory for the answers that she wasn't sure she could find.

"No, he just stopped worrying. He didn't say much, but then, Gary didn't always say much. He was sure that getting rich quick was always around the corner." She stopped, half of her sandwich suspended in one hand. "No, wait. He did say something. Something a little odd. He asked if I knew where his old notebooks from school were, if I'd be able to find them if he needed them.''

''And you said?'' Hank leaned even farther in.

''That they were probably in the storage space we rented over in Union. And he made sure that I had the key on my key ring, not just lying around someplace.''

Gloria looked at Hank. ''Sounds like we have a trip to make. And then some calls.'' She looked at Lori, and Lori felt as if she was being measured for a task. ''How are you at cards? Specifically poker?''

For the first time since they sat down at the Town Hall, Lori felt a little uneasy. ''I've never played. But why do I get the feeling you're asking about something else?''

Gloria nodded. ''You're right. I am. It's pretty obvious that Clyde is up to no good. And I can tell from what he hasn't said that Hank suspects he may have had plenty to do with your husband's death.''

Hank grimaced. ''And I still can't say anything, Gloria. Not for certain.''

''But it's possible,'' Lori said, feeling herself start to shake.

Hank nodded. ''And there's one way to find out for sure. That's where those poker-playing skills would come in. We could set a trap for Hughes.''

It was becoming clearer. ''With me as bait?'' When Hank nodded again, Lori wondered if she was really up to what these two had in mind.

Chapter Twelve

Mike looked at her suspiciously when she went back to the office. Lori was sure of it. She tried to act as nonchalant as possible when Gloria dropped her off in the nearest parking lot and she walked back the four doors to the office. But Mike's normally friendly gaze looked less friendly than usual this time.

"Have a good time?" He wanted more than a simple yes or no for an answer, Lori was sure.

"Fine." Lori busied herself settling the baby in her crib.

"What are you up to with those two, anyway?" Mike crossed the room, and Lori's temper flared.

She didn't have to answer his questions. There was no reason that anything that went on in the

Town Hall was Mike's business. "Nothing. We just had lunch. Why do you ask?"

Mike stopped, his lifted eyebrows telling her he seemed to be taken aback by her quick, sharp response. "Sorry I asked. It's just that this isn't a normal occurrence. You going out to lunch, I mean, especially with Hank and my mom."

"Well, I did go today. And I might even do it again." She changed the baby while she spoke, unwilling to look into Mike's face. She could hide their plans from him if she was looking down at Mikayla instead, but probably not if she looked at his handsome, honest face.

Did this pang of guilt mean she was wrong for concealing their plans from him? Lori made sure Mikayla was put back together well, socks snug enough that she couldn't pull them off for a few minutes and gently turned her over on her tummy to play and rock in the crib.

"Why are you so concerned about who I have lunch with, anyway?" she asked.

Mike's expression went from curious to stubborn. "I'm not concerned. Not that much. It's not like I'm jealous of Hank Collins or anything. With either of you, I might add."

Why didn't his words convince her? His expression didn't do much more to make her feel at ease.

Brow furrowed, hands jammed in his pockets, Mike looked like a man trying not to argue.

"You sure about all that?" She tried to keep her tone of voice light. It was aggravating that she almost wanted him to admit that he was just a bit jealous. Or worried about what she might be doing having lunch with Hank and Gloria. Instead, he just seemed curious and perhaps a bit anxious about his mother.

"Positive." Mike rocked back on his heels. "Where'd the two of them get to? I didn't expect you back alone."

"Well, that's what you got." Mike felt very near now, and challenging. "They went their own ways. Hank had to go back to the office, and your mom went to pick up some documents at the courthouse. She said you'd remember that part."

Mike sighed. "Trust me to forget. Sorry for giving you the third degree, Lori. It's just that I'm not used to worrying about my mom and what she's doing. Or you, either, for that matter. I'm usually the one who goes out for lunch. Did you know there were seven phone calls while you were gone?"

Lori shrugged. "That's about normal." It felt like a letdown, knowing he wasn't really concerned. For a moment she considered telling him about their planned meeting tomorrow at the storage facility. That might concern him.

She decided against it. This was an exercise to clear Gary's name of any suspicion, and to see if they could lay any blame at Clyde Hughes's door instead. It was something she needed to do without Mike. Something she needed to do for the sake of her children so that someday when they asked about their father, she could tell them the truth.

She hoped they'd find what Hank expected in that storage facility. Or find nothing that incriminated Gary, at least. She wanted to believe everything he'd told her in the year before his death. That his one arrest for drug-related behavior had been a terrible mistake on his part. That he would never dream of getting involved with anything like that again.

Still, what other way would he have had to make big money quick when he went off that last morning, confident that their finances were suddenly going to be straightened out? Lori's head ached contemplating that.

"You all right?" Mike was a step closer. He truly looked concerned by now. "Are you dizzy or something?"

Lori shook her head, then wished she hadn't. "Not dizzy. Just a little headache. I'll be fine, really. Now tell me about those phone calls. Anything I can do to ease the workload?''

Mike cupped her elbow in his hand and steered her to her office chair. Instead of feeling manhandled, Lori felt taken care of. ''I'd still be happier if you sat down. You look a little pale. And I've seen enough people pass out during fire-and-rescue missions to know the signs. I don't want to have to catch you. Although it might be fun.'' His grin had a touch of wolf or coyote to it. But friendly.

Lori couldn't help but grin back. ''I'm sure it might be. For you. Now, the phone calls, Michael?''

Settling her in her chair, he grimaced a bit. ''Michael? Oh, joy. Now I really *am* on your bad side. I have got to stop letting you hang out with my mother.''

''Try and stop me.'' Lori was sure her smile was as sweet as possible. Mike rolled his eyes and reached for the stack of sticky notes with their phone messages.

Mike had been watching Lori for days. There was definitely something going on with her. Mike watched her across the office. She seemed a little off her normal hectic pace. Tyler was done with school and sat at an empty desk, happily coloring while his mother worked and Mikayla slept. Usually she only stayed a short time once Tyler came from school, and then she was done. Today, and for the last couple of days, ever since she'd had lunch with Hank and his mother, she had been staying longer and looking a little flustered.

Maybe *flustered* wasn't quite the right word. Mike watched her for a while longer, trying to find the correct description. Lori seemed as well put together as usual. But she wasn't smiling as often as she normally did. And she seemed to hold Mikayla much more tightly when she rocked her. They were little things, but put together, they worried Mike.

How had he let this woman and her family get close enough to worry him in such a short time? Because she did worry him, at every opportunity. If it wasn't concern for what was going on with Lori, it was the anticipation of seeing her again or trying to figure out how she'd stretch her limited wardrobe yet another way to come up with another flattering outfit.

She was constantly in his thoughts when she wasn't right there in front of him. Surely this had to stop. Even when he was out on his rare fire-and-rescue calls, he was anxious to get back to the office, or the house, where he could catch a glimpse of Lori. And nothing had ever taken his attention from fire-and-rescue work before.

Even Dogg seemed to notice the change. Often

when Mike was ready to take him for his evening walk around the property, he found the big shepherd staring out the glass patio doors in the kitchen facing Lori's house. ''We'll stop there last,'' Mike always told him, and he was good to his word. Dogg got a biscuit from Tyler and attention from Lori, and he got a last good-night. He wondered who enjoyed those meetings more. It probably wasn't Dogg.

The phone rang and Lori actually jumped. That did it. Mike stood up from his desk to see what was going on. Before he could cross the room, Lori was talking on the phone, and seemed to have gotten over being startled. He could tell from her end of the conversation that it was some kind of inquiry on a vacant store near the edge of town.

Whatever Lori had expected, this wasn't it. She put the phone back in the cradle and smiled at him. Was it his imagination, or did her smile slightly waver? ''Did you want something?''

''Definitely. But I don't think I can get it here in the office.'' Oh, how incredibly stale. Mike winced internally. Was that really the best answer he could come up with? She must be sure by now that he was a total cretin. ''Let's start over. That didn't come out the way I'd planned it.''

Lori was stifling a giggle. ''Good. Because it did

sound pretty odd. Now, what can I do for you, Mike?''

"Go out to lunch with me. Without Hank, or my mother, or anybody else. Except Mikayla, of course.''

"Of course. I don't think your mother would appreciate being left to man the phones and watch the baby at the same time. Is tomorrow soon enough?''

"Sure. Unless you'd rather sweet-talk Mom into taking Tyler home to feed the goats while we go to a movie in Washington tonight instead. If we hustle, we could catch the five-thirty show.''

Lori's brow wrinkled. "That sounds suspiciously like a date, even with the baby along.''

Mike shrugged. "Maybe it is. You look awful harried lately. I figured you could use some time alone, or at least a little side trip with popcorn for dinner.''

Lori's laugh was musical. It moved Mike in places he didn't know existed inside of him. "I really could use a break. And you figured out without me even asking. Neat. My first little miracle of the day.''

"You use that phrase a lot. Miracles. Do you really believe in them?'' Suddenly, knowing was important, even if it meant that Lori would decide not to go on their date this evening.

"I really do. My grandmother always said miracles exist all around us. That you could find at least a dozen every day if you weren't picky about size.''

"And do you? Find a dozen a day, I mean?"

Her brow wrinkled. "Not a whole dozen every day. But I figure there's so many stored up for me already in heaven that I'm probably at least a week ahead.''

"At a dozen a day, that's a lot of miracles. And you really believe all that, don't you? How can it be so simple?''

"Now this is what I was trying to explain to you at Christmas. Except I did a poor job of it then, and I'm probably not going to do much better now. Take a seat. This may take a few minutes.''

Mike sighed. "Are we still going to the movies?''

Lori grinned at him, and patted the chair next to hers. "Yes, I think we are.''

He sat while she rearranged the pencils on her desk. "It's not that I don't want to believe. It's just that you make this whole faith thing look so easy. And I know for a fact that nothing in this life is that easy. You have to work for things, plan them.''

"Anticipate them?" Lori put down the pencils. "Working with the fire-and-rescue team, you have to anticipate a lot, don't you?''

"If you don't, you may not last long. There are

just too many things that could do you in. A falling beam, a backdraft you didn't expect, one of a million things.''

''I don't know much about fire fighting. Do you have to do that all alone?''

Mike leaned toward her. He could talk about this for hours. He wasn't sure what it had to do with faith, but it was at least a subject he was comfortable with. ''You're never totally alone. No firefighter goes into a building without a lifeline, oxygen, communication.''

''And somebody running the show is outside on the truck, or nearby, right?''

''For somebody who doesn't know much about this, you pick up fast.'' Lori blushed at his compliment. Mike savored the rosy glow her cheeks got. ''But what has this got to do with how simple your life is?''

''Everything. Don't you see it's the same way with Jesus? You're never alone. It doesn't mean you don't have to think for yourself, or anticipate things. But it does mean that no matter where you are, and what you're doing, He's there with you. Jesus is my lifeline, Mike. And he could be yours, too. All you need to do is ask.''

''I don't know if I'm ready to do that. But this explanation makes a lot more sense than the one you tried on Christmas.''

"Yeah, well, I know you better now. Maybe I know how to talk to you. Now tell me one of the important things about you. Do you or do you not like that awful slimy fake butter stuff on your movie popcorn?"

Mike laughed. He couldn't help it. "Put that way, there's only one right answer to that question. We'll get the popcorn plain. That is, if we can talk Mom into taking Tyler."

"It shouldn't be a problem. As long as we take Mikayla, I think we're home free. Let's go ask."

Lori stood up and reached out for his hand. It felt natural to take hers to walk across the office to his mother's door. He still didn't know quite what was bothering her, but somehow Mike felt that he had a much better chance finding out in a darkened movie theater. Especially if holding hands with her during the movie felt as good as it did now. The lady had hands like warm satin.

Lori wasn't sure if it was the popcorn and the box of candy for dinner, or the lighthearted comedy, or the fact that Mike didn't seem at all bothered by going to the movies with a nearly-two-month-old, that endeared him to her more than usual. Even when Mikayla got a little hungry and fussy she managed from their seat, far back in the theater, to feed her inconspicuously. Her angel baby even burped quietly, not disturbing the other movie patrons.

The theater wasn't very crowded, and the manager had laughed at Lori's offer to buy Mikayla a ticket so that she would feel right about putting the infant carrier in a seat instead of down on the awful floor. That and Mike's good-natured teasing about taking the baby on a date got them all laughing.

Mike held her hand almost all the time when she wasn't feeding the baby. It might have been the most romantic date she'd ever been on. Seeing that it hadn't started out as a real date at all, but just a spur-of-the-moment thing, she felt grateful. When Mike suggested a detour for ice cream to top off their nutritious popcorn-and-candy dinner, what could she say but yes?

"You have hot fudge on your nose," he told her a bit later as they shared a banana split at the Dairy Delight.

Her heart skipped a beat as he took a napkin and wiped the offending spot. He was smiling about the whole thing, and Lori's resolve melted with the ice cream. "I have to tell you something," she blurted.

Before she said anything else, Mike's expression got serious. "You can tell me anything, as long as it's not that you won't go out with me again. I had way too much fun tonight for this to be our first *and* last date."

She nearly dropped her spoon in surprise. "No. That's not it at all. I'd love to do this three or four nights a week if it didn't mean leaving Tyler, and slowing down on the work I bring home."

He brightened. "You would? Really?"

"Really. But that isn't what I wanted to say. It's about my lunch with your mom and Hank."

Mike's brow furrowed. How was she going to get this man to start thinking positively? It surely wasn't part of his nature. "Please don't tell me they're running off to Vegas."

"You never cease to amaze me. Think good thoughts for a change, Michael," she said softly. "They might be planning to run off, but I doubt those two would go to Vegas or Reno, or anyplace like that. If I know them at all it would be someplace like the Precious Moments Chapel in Springfield. But no, our lunch was mostly business. Business you aren't going to like."

Mike looked surprised, still holding the folded napkin he'd used on her face. "But you're going to tell me anyway? Even though you know I won't like it?"

"I am. Not that I'll let you do anything besides tell me you don't like it. I'm still going to do what Hank wants me to do. But I can't keep you in the dark anymore. You're becoming too important to me to leave you out."

For once she couldn't read his expression. His handsome face was a mystery to her. Lori took a deep breath. Once she told him about the plan to trap Clyde Hughes, Mike would be no mystery. He'd be close to two hundred pounds of angry, protective male, and she had no idea how to handle that. But she was going to try.

Grandma always said God never gave you more than He could handle with you. It was folks who decided that God never gave them more than they could handle on their own that got in trouble. She breathed a silent prayer. *Gran, I really hope you're right this time.*

An hour later Mike was dropping her off at the door to the little green house. "I still don't like this," he told her, watching her shoo Tyler into the house and set the infant seat, with Mikayla napping again, inside on the carpet.

"I know that. And thank you for telling me instead of assuming you have some right to forbid me to do it. Because I have to do it."

"For Gary?"

"More for the kids. And a little for Gary. And pretty much for myself, to get some peace out of this, some closure. And I'll keep your present right next to me all the time."

Mike looked down at her large bag, part handbag, part diaper bag, holding everything she needed to carry around. "Good. I don't believe in carrying concealed weapons, even if it was legal in Missouri. But you can be sure that anytime you're not in sight of me, I'm going to have that two-way radio on, and I want you to do the same."

"I will. And thank you again, Mike."

His arms were around her now. She could hear Tyler giggling from inside the doorway. This was important to him. Hey, who was she kidding? It was important for her, too. "Anytime. I need to keep all of you safe. If this is the only way you'll let me do it, this is what I'll deal with. Pleasant dreams."

He leaned down and kissed her softly. Lori could feel his shoulder muscles tighten beneath her fingers as Tyler's giggles erupted into peals of laughter. "And what's so funny?" Mike demanded, looking at her son.

"Kissing?" Tyler was nearly falling over with laughter. "That's as girlie as thinking babies are cute."

"The baby *is* cute. And someday you'll think kissing isn't 'girlie' at all. But for now, you have it your way, Tyler." Mike released her and winked, telling them all good-night. Lori watched him cross the darkness between the houses, then shut the door.

This felt better. Telling Mike had been the right thing to do, and his reaction had been the biggest miracle of the day. *Thank You* was all she could whisper as she locked the door and started to get the children ready for bed. *Thank You so much for bringing this man into my life.*

Chapter Thirteen

Hank wasn't happy with Lori for telling Mike about their plans. "It's not that I don't trust him. It's just that the fewer people know anything about this, the better it will work."

"I couldn't not tell him. If that makes sense to you," Lori said. They sat in the Martin office in plain view, where it looked like they could be going over city ordinances or permits of any kind that Martin Properties could need to lease something.

Instead they were looking at Gary's college notebooks, retrieved from the storage facility in Washington. Lori had forgotten the amount of stuff they'd put in the small locker. It was fun to find the box of Tyler's baby clothes that she'd forgotten they kept. It was disturbing to find Gary's note-books.

That box had been easy to find. It was on top of a stack and, unlike all the others, was dusted clean and had been recently opened. Directly on top was a binder marked ''Chemistry 250'' that had a sticky note attached to the front with her name written on it.

Lori's hands still shook when she looked at the contents. In among the perfectly innocent notes for an organic chemistry class, Gary had interspersed records of loads of supplies going in and out of the feed store in large quantities.

Much of what he detailed could be used to make farm fertilizer. However, when combined with a few other perfectly legal substances, Hank pointed out that the chemicals and ingredients in his notes could also make methamphetamines.

''It looks like Clyde hired your husband for a purpose, and put you all up on that land for the same reason,'' Hank said after he'd leafed through the notebook. ''Knowing Gary's previous record, he figured that he could nail him with the meth lab and the supplies if any of it was found.''

''But Gary caught on first and was going to blackmail Hughes instead. I'm not sure that makes me happier than the thought that he was making drugs.'' Lori stared down at the metal desktop. ''I guess I'm glad that he didn't do either one in the end.''

"And just the idea of blackmailing Hughes cost him his life. After seeing this, I'm pretty sure Hughes drugged your husband and drowned him. Now we have to prove that. What we've got here wouldn't hold up for a grand jury. However, it wouldn't take much more to get an indictment. All we need is one solid link showing Hughes is aware of the contents of this notebook and the supplies going in and out of the feed store.''

"And I guess you need me to provide that." Lori looked at Hank. He looked like somebody's father again, concerned for her safety.

"I hate to admit it, but yes, we do," he said. "This is not the way I wanted to do things. Involving somebody like you, with no law-enforcement background, with two little children, is just about my last choice.''

"It is the logical choice, though," Lori said softly. "And the one that Mr. Hughes is least likely to suspect. I mean he pretty much thinks of me as this helpless girl depending on someone to rescue her. If I call him, hinting that he could buy some information off me and I could go away and start over someplace, he'd take that bait.''

"I suspect so. But he's capable of a lot. We can't

underestimate him. I hate to admit it, but in the long run you probably did the right thing telling Mike.''

"I know I did. God left me no doubt of that when we were in the theater last night.''

Hank split a grin that made him look much less concerned. ''Now that's an interesting place for such a revelation. Not that I don't believe it could happen that way. I've gotten some of my clearest messages from the Man Upstairs in some awfully unlikely places.''

"I'm not sure any more that there's such a thing as an unlikely place for a message from Him.'' Lori smiled back. ''And this one was pretty clear. Mike belongs in on this one, even though it complicates things.''

"He'll be a good man to have around if the going gets tough. But then you already know that,'' Hank said.

Lori hoped she didn't blush too deeply. It was one of those uncontrollable things that she wished she could change about herself. Mike had already told her he thought it was cute. She thought it made her look about fourteen. Oh, well, she wasn't that much a woman of the world to begin with. Might as well accept the fact that she wasn't going to be cool and collected under pressure.

She could be as calm as possible. And to do that, they needed to plan out what she would do and say on the phone with Hughes. "So explain to me just how to do this," she told Hank. "I want this particular chapter in my life closed as soon as we can get it that way."

"Consider it done." He leaned over the notebooks and spoke quietly. "Now this will be the last time I can see you in public for a while without stirring up that weasel's suspicions. So let's get it all worked out…"

Why had he ever agreed to this? Mike paced around his apartment, two-way radio still in hand. He was going to wear a path in the carpet if he didn't slow down. He'd go into the main house and wear a path in his mother's carpet, but he didn't want her to know how deeply he was involved in this whole mess.

How could she have let Lori get involved with a plan to catch scum like Hughes? Mike knew that if confronted, his mother would not see things the same way he did. In her eyes, Lori was a competent young woman, able to take care of herself in almost any situation. Gloria's growing trust in her regarding the business showed him that.

She was probably right. But it made Mike sweat to think of tiny Lori, alone in the world, taking on a powerful guy like Hughes, even once, to spring a trap. Why didn't he tell her not to do it?

He stopped pacing. Because he had no right to tell her anything of the kind, that's why. One kiss and one date did not give a guy enough say-so in a woman's life to forbid her to do something like this. He should be grateful that she agreed to the two-way radios. "Still awake over there?" he couldn't resist asking into his.

There was a crackle of static, and then a soft laugh. "Of course. I just put the kids down for the last time not ten minutes ago. It's only nine o'clock. Do you think I go to bed with the chickens?"

Mike was tempted to tell her what he really thought: he wished she could be with him. Not for the pleasure it would bring them, but for the protection he could give her. He didn't dare say that, however. "I still wish we would have tapped the phone over there."

"Not legal. Hank said there was no way he could get an order for a wiretap, and we couldn't use one in a court of law any other way."

"Yeah, but I'd like to have it in hard evidence if that guy threatens you or comes on to you or anything."

"He might threaten me, but I doubt he'd do anything. Mike, he's old enough to be my father. And he's a very successful man in this community. Why would he risk all that over somebody like me?"

It was on the tip of his tongue to tell Lori just how precious ''somebody like her'' could be. But Mike had no idea how to say what he wanted to, so he left it for now. ''You keep that radio where I can hear your end of the call, at least.''

''Will do. Now tell me good-night so I can go make the call. And pray for me, will you?''

''Sure.'' He didn't know if he could. Didn't know what good it would do if he did pray for her, or even for himself. But Mike wasn't about to tell Lori that over this two-way radio, or even in person. So he put things on standby mode to listen in while she called Hughes. And he sat down in his favorite leather recliner to listen.

Dogg padded over and put one huge front paw on his knee. ''Later,'' he told the beast, rubbing his head. ''We'll walk, as soon as this is over.'' The dog gave a gusty canine sigh and dropped to the floor. He knew the word *later* and wasn't too fond of it. But he didn't argue.

Mike told himself that if he had Lori's mind-set he'd call that a little miracle. Maybe the first one in a series, if this call went okay. But he wasn't far enough along to call anything a miracle yet. He was sure God had a few of them up His sleeve, but he hadn't shown many to him yet. Time would have to tell.

* * *

One ring. Two rings. Someone picked up the phone at Hughes's number. "Hello?"

"Mr. Hughes?"

"Yes. Who's calling?" His voice was smooth, cultured. Lori was ready to hang up right then and call it a night. Surely she couldn't do this. *Help, Lord!*

She took a deep breath. Time to concentrate. Time to steady her hands and her voice. "This is Lori Harper. Gary's wife?" She tried to sound even more breathy and scatterbrained than she felt. In her half-panicky state, it was easy.

"Right. What can I do for you, Lori?"

Here it went. She wished she'd written everything down, like a script, once she and Hank planned it all in the office. But then it would probably sound rehearsed. No, this was better, even though her heart was racing and her hand was almost too damp to hold the phone. "I, uh, seem to have something of yours. Or at least something with your name on it."

There was a short pause. "I don't know how that could be. Unless it's something you found at the trailer, perhaps, that I'd left there."

He was taking the bait. "No, that's not it, Mr. Hughes. You see, I was cleaning out our storage space yesterday. The rent on the space was due, and I decided I couldn't afford it anymore."

"I suspect money is rather tight for you, even working at Martin Properties like you are." He sounded so smooth, so positively *oily*. Lori's stomach flipped while she planned out what to say next.

"You know it is. Anyway, I found some of Gary's old things. One batch of papers seems to be from work. They certainly mention your name often. I thought you might want to have them, uh, for your records."

"And naturally you intend to just pop by the feed store tomorrow and give them to me for free." Hughes's voice had a cynical edge now.

"Well, like you said, things are kind of tight. And if I'm going to move down to Sedalia with the kids like I've planned, there's a few things I'll need."

"Naturally. These papers... How often do they mention my name?"

Hughes was getting more interested. This wasn't a direct admission that he was doing anything illegal, but if he was totally innocent, why would he care what kind of paperwork Gary Harper had left behind?

Lori felt a pang of remorse for ever thinking Gary had gone back on his promise to her that he wasn't involved in illegal drug trafficking. From his perspective, he hadn't been involved. He probably even saw this all as a favor to the police and the county, getting a drug lab shut down.

"Well, you do seem to be in there a lot. Gary even said something about your plans to expand the business."

"Oh?" Hughes's intake of breath was sharp. "What kind of expansion?"

"It looks like pharmacy work to me, Mr. Hughes. That or somebody in your family certainly gets a lot of bad colds." Lori let out her breath, trying to remember to focus and feel less light-headed. This was going just the way Hank had said it would. And Hughes wasn't denying the link to the other ingredients for the meth lab.

There was a pause on Hughes's end of the line while Lori held her breath. "I'm sure I could convince you of the perfect legality of all those purchases." Good. This was getting closer. "And you say you have the paperwork there with you?"

"I do now."

"You haven't shown it to anybody, have you? I'd hate for something like that, which could be misconstrued so easily, to fall into the wrong hands." Did Hughes sound nervous, or was it just a slightly bad phone connection?

"Of course not. Why would I show it to anybody but you, Mr. Hughes? I can't think of anyone else who would be interested. Unless, of course, this is something else besides just a list of business supplies…"

"Which it isn't," Hughes was quick to reply. "Perhaps we could go to lunch together tomorrow. Maybe even with your delightful children. Would you like that, Mrs. Harper?"

"We can leave the kids out of this." Her response was natural, but quick. "This just involves the two of us, Mr. Hughes. And I look forward to hearing from you again. Soon." She hung up, willing her hands not to shake.

It only took about thirty seconds after the connection was broken for her radio across the room to crackle to life. "Okay, fill in his end of the conversation," Mike growled. "I want every detail. There is no way I'll get to sleep tonight unless I know what's going on first."

Lori picked up her handset. "Fine. For once I'm glad you're worried about me. Let me run it all by you and see what you think."

Mike found himself tossing and turning. He had dozed off several times, only to wake up and listen to the night sounds around the place. Lori and the kids should really be back in his mom's guest room in the main house. Or he and Dogg ought to be over there. Granted, either situation would blow everything if Hughes or someone working for him came nosing around.

But it was hard to justify the sheriff's investigation of Hughes as being more important than Lori Harper and her kids. They were becoming more precious to him every day, and he didn't want to jeopardize their safety even for a moment.

How had that happened? He didn't think of himself as a family man, exactly. Yet, here he was with a beautiful young woman often by his side, and her with two small kids. It boggled the mind. The roughest part of the whole situation was that even though he had a good job, more money than he knew what to do with and could meet her every need financially, she probably wouldn't have anything to do with him in the long run because he wasn't a Christian.

That was not exactly true. He believed in God, just not in the intensely personal way Lori seemed to. It was beyond his understanding to trust the way she did. Suddenly chilled, Mike pulled up the blankets.

His being cold was only partly due to the open window. His mother would skin him alive if she knew he was sleeping with the window open this early in March, even to hear what was going on outside. Still, he wasn't comfortable doing things any other way, so it was a good thing his apartment was on zoned heating and away from his mother's bedroom.

Having the windows open made him happier with the fact that his apartment was probably as far as you could get from that little green house and not leave the property. For once he wished he had a good, direct view of the place. There was always another check-in on the two-way radio. He could see it outlined on his bedside table.

Mike couldn't quite bring himself to turn it on again. Surely he was the only one worrying like this. Lori was asleep, with those kids down for the night hours ago. He would only disturb her if he called again now.

Before he could reach for the radio, Dogg whined on the floor at his feet. "Come on. Come tell me all about it." Mike patted the side of his bed, expecting the dog to pad up to the head of the bed and complain. Instead, the beast's ears perked up and he stood. This wasn't a particularly good sign.

Dogg stayed focused on something outside. Mike got up and looked out the window. It took a moment for his eyes to get used to the dark. He couldn't see anything different at the one corner of the green house he could see from this angle. But then…from the bushes near the corner of the house it seemed a deeper shadow detached itself from the shadows there for a split second.

Everything happened at once. Dogg's whining gave way to a full-throated growl, and the shadow definitely became the shape of a person. There was the crash of glass and a woman's scream, and a roaring whoosh as the darkness was lit by flames.

The radio on his bedside crackled to life as Mike struggled into jeans, groping for shoes. "Mike. Help. Something just happened. I think the house is on fire."

"I'll call the crew and I'll be right there. All of you get out of that house, now!" Mike shut off the radio and reached for the phone to get his 911 call made.

He had to make the call to get the trucks here as soon as possible. But that meant losing the chance of catching whoever threw the device that caused the fire. He swore under his breath. Catching the bad guy was key, but getting Lori, Tyler and Mikayla out of that house was far more important.

Dressed now, with shoes on, he barked instructions into the phone. Once she knew who it was, the dispatcher told him to hang up so he could go be more useful at the fire scene instead of staying on the line until the fire-and-rescue vehicles came. That was good, because Mike wouldn't have stayed there anyway. He threw down the phone and bolted from his apartment. Every second counted, as he knew all too well. He'd faced a lot of situations like this before, but not with people he cared about battling the flames. Not for a very long time. Running toward the green house, he broke out in a cold sweat.

Chapter Fourteen

This was a waking nightmare. Smoke billowed in the hall as Lori ran with the screaming baby. "Tyler. Come on now. I need you with me now," she called into the dark hallway, which was growing darker as the smoke grew.

"Mama?" Tyler was coughing. How awful for a little child to be awakened from a sound sleep by fire and smoke in his own home. That horrified Lori more than her own experience. It was hard to remember which way to go in all this confusion.

"Here I am, Ty. Come out in the hall and hurry. We need to get out of here." In a moment his solid body ran into hers and Lori nearly burst into tears of gratitude. Clutching his hand, she groped her way down the hall to the kitchen door. There would be no going through the front door. Whatever had started the fire had begun in the living room. The furniture was burning and the drapes had caught. Going into that room was impossible.

The kitchen wasn't burning yet, but dense smoke had begun to fill the room. After struggling with the unfamiliar locks for a moment, they were out in the fresh air, gulping it.

What had happened back there? One moment, everybody was in bed, asleep, and the next there was a horrible noise of shattering glass and the living room was on fire. Someone had to have thrown something through the window. That, or someone had actually been inside the house and set the fire. Either possibility made Lori light-headed. It was hard to think of even Clyde Hughes as being that coldhearted when small children were involved.

Tyler was wide-eyed and Mikayla was still sobbing. Lori jostled the baby on her shoulder, grateful that they were all in one piece and outside. "Let's move away from the house and go toward Mike's house, okay? I don't want smoke to get in our eyes," she told Tyler, tugging him gently away from the house.

"Are the fire engines coming?" Tyler looked up at her.

"Soon. Very soon," Lori promised, praying that it was true. It would take a huge blaze and plenty of wind for anything else on the property, except her beaten-up old car, to be in danger, but it was always possible. If the firefighters got here soon, she would feel a lot better. She strained to hear sirens.

"Will they need mine? Mom?" Tyler pulled on her arm. "Where's my fire engine?"

Lori tried to pay attention to Tyler's question. It surprised her that he was worried about a toy, even his favorite one. "Inside, I guess, sweetheart. We just got the important things, like people." Lori realized with a pang that none of them had any clothes except for what they had slept in. For her that was old flannel boxers and a T-shirt, and for the kids it was pajamas. Tyler didn't even have shoes.

He broke away from her grasp, yelling, "I need my fire engine. Mike will need it. I have to get my fire engine so we can help."

"No, Tyler. That's a toy, and we have to just leave it for now. We have to go, Tyler. Now. Don't go there," Lori shrieked, running, but he broke away from her and went back into the house.

Her screaming made Mikayla cry louder. Lori stood at the door of the house, stunned. She couldn't take the baby back in there. But she couldn't leave Tyler inside, either.

Mike running across the grass was a vision. He

was truly her guardian angel this time. "Mike, Tyler went back inside. He said he had to get his fire engine. I couldn't stop him. What do we do?"

He looked grim. Pushing her away from the door, back into the grass, Mike looked toward his apartment. "The trucks are on their way. But my oxygen and equipment are on one of those trucks. There's no time to wait for it. Where would he be?"

"Heading for his bedroom. At least it's away from where the fire started. But the smoke was so thick..." Lori felt tears streaming down her face. Mike put his hands on her shoulders, steering her farther from the house again.

"There's no sense in telling you to go up to the house and sit with my mom. You won't move any farther from here until I come out with Tyler." He headed toward the house. "Keep Dogg out here with you. Don't let him follow me into that fire, no matter what."

"I'll try," Lori promised, reaching down for the animal's collar. He whined, but didn't growl or snap, even though he wanted to follow his master. She pulled the dog to her side and they huddled together in the grass as far away from the house as she dared get. And she prayed as she had never prayed before while two of the people most precious to her in the world were in terrible, terrible trouble. For the present they were truly in God's hands.

He couldn't do this. Mike Martin stood just inside the kitchen door to the house, scanning the area for movement besides the roiling smoke. Where was Tyler? Could the boy even figure out the way to his bedroom in this mess?

Once inside, there wasn't much choice of a path except to the bedrooms. The front of the house was an inferno. Tyler wouldn't have gone to the basement, so he had to have headed into the bedrooms.

It was as if giant hands pushed him back, kept him from moving. Mike had never liked going into a house on fire. Some of the guys claimed to, but it had always been his least favorite situation. And this particular time, fear and something else even more elemental had him rooted to the spot.

I can't do this. The words screamed in his brain while the smoke choked him. Was he going to be able to walk outside and tell Lori that? If they waited for the trucks to get there and somebody with proper gear to go after Tyler, it would probably be too late. At the very least he would suffer smoke inhalation and probably some burns.

Still not moving forward, Mike dropped to his knees. Smoke rose, so the best air, if there was any, would be nearer the floor. That was beginner's knowledge, something he should have remembered, and done, first thing.

His perspective matched Tyler's from down here. And it dawned on him that it also matched Lori's, not in real height, where she at least came to his collarbone or better. But in her trust and faith, she always seemed to be on her knees, talking to God.

She was praying for him and for Tyler right now. Mike knew that without even wondering. Knowing of her resolve, Mike made a decision himself. It was time for him to call upon that Lord that Lori held so dear.

He spoke the words out loud as smoke gagged him. "Lord, I haven't been much of a believer. And maybe it's wrong to come to You now when I need help so badly. But I can't do this on my own. Help me find Tyler."

He was on his hands and knees now, crawling through the dark area. The floor was smooth, so it was still kitchen vinyl tile. Or did the hallway continue in the same stuff? Mike racked his brain trying to remember. The layout of the small house was so familiar that he didn't have to question where each room was. That was a blessing, maybe even one of those miracles Lori always talked about. He was going to need several to get out of here in one piece with Tyler. Especially when he couldn't be sure what the floor in each room was made out of, and in the hellish atmosphere around him, floor texture was his only guide.

The surface under his fingers was still smooth. Continuing to move forward, he swept the area as widely as possible with his fingertips. In front of him he hit wall and baseboards. He was in the hall. That meant he needed a left turn to reach the bedrooms. *Thank you, Jesus.* It was good to get this far and to know where he was.

One doorway, on the right. That would be the bathroom. That meant that Tyler's room should be there on the left, just a few more feet down. He swept the area with his fingers again and found another break in the wall. The smoke was almost overpowering now, and the noise of the fire incredible.

"Tyler? You in there?" he called. There was no answer. Mike crawled into the room and raised up on his knees. He could see next to nothing. Shapes and shadows were the only landmarks in the dank smoke. In the corner was a shape that was probably the dresser. Closet doors gaped open and he reached inside. He found shoes, toys, but no little boy.

Coughing again, he backed out into the room. He had to find Tyler soon and get out of here. Their survival depended on it. Across from the closet, flanking another wall was a twin bed. He remembered that from being in the house after Lori moved in. The room wasn't large, only five or six steps of free space between the closet and bed. He shuffled on his knees over to the bed.

Mike could feel covers flung back and puddling on the floor. Strong instinct made him delve into the blankets on the floor. Wasn't this where he would hide if he were a little kid in this situation? If not in the closet, under the bed was the ''safest'' place in your room. That was the way a little boy would think. It was the way he was being urged to think now. He could only thank God silently for the guidance while he groped.

At the corner of the bed he felt something warm and soft. It was a small foot, and he followed the path up to sturdy legs, hauling Tyler out from under the bed.

''Mike?'' The child was only semiconscious. ''I gotta have my fire engine.''

He had to cough for quite a while before he could answer the child he gathered in his arms. ''Okay, buddy. I'll grab it and you. Then we're getting out of here. Come on.'' Outwardly all he could do was choke on the fumes and smoke around them, but inwardly Mike was praising the God he had only found in this inferno of smoke and flames for leading him to Tyler. Now He had to get them out of here and to the child's mother. Breathing in a silent prayer, Mike knew that He was the only one who could do it.

They had been in there forever. Lori couldn't believe how long it had been since Mike went into that house. Gloria was sitting next to her, holding Mikayla and trying to comfort her. Right now Gloria was doing a better job than she could have done herself.

Dogg was leashed and fastened to a tree next to them. If he pulled much harder, he was going to snap the metal lead or uproot the tree, she was sure. Barking and whining, he pulled with his whole body toward the house. Lori didn't even try to quiet him because she felt the same way. She wanted to go in there with all her being, and only knowing that she would be absolutely no help kept her sitting on the ground, wrapped in the blanket Gloria had brought her.

Her prayers were constant and almost mindless. She couldn't form coherent words anymore, just powerful thoughts of protection for Tyler and Mike. The house didn't matter, but the people certainly did. Could they really come out all right after that much time in a burning building?

There were firefighters here now, Carrie among them. She was standing over Lori, shaking her shoulder. "Where's Mike? And where's your little boy?"

"Tyler ran back in the house. Mike went after him. They've been gone too long…" Lori choked out. She had run out of words. Carrie looked toward the house.

"I've got to alert the captain we have people in there. Whoa, people coming out." She launched herself toward the doorway, nearly obscured in black, oily smoke, where Lori could see a figure charging through.

It was Mike, with a limp Tyler under one arm and that darned fire engine that started it all clutched in the other hand. He only made it a few feet out into the grass before he loosed his precious burdens and fell to his knees.

Carrie was there to pick up Tyler and scream for others to help the two of them. In a flash the crew moved Mike and Tyler farther away from the house and there were medical personnel checking them both out.

Lori wanted to hold her boy, thank Mike for risking his life, talk to them both. But she held back at the edge of the crowd to let the paramedics do their job.

Were they both alive? All right? Her heart hammered in her throat as she searched the scene for clues. They were both sooty, but appeared to be breathing. As she watched, one of the men quickly picked Tyler up and moved him into a sitting position where he choked and retched. "Mama! I want my mom!" he called.

Lori couldn't stand being away from him any longer. She pushed her way through the onlookers. "I'm here, Ty. Now do whatever the doctors tell you, okay. Don't fight them." He was conscious now and struggling, and she stroked his face. His skin was smooth and unburned. "Is he okay?" she asked the nearest paramedic softly.

"I think so. He needs oxygen, for sure. We've got to get him stable, but I don't think he's been burned any." He looked at Lori. "I'm going to take him over to the truck. Come with me."

She nodded, looking over to where two other paramedics worked over Mike. "We need oxygen here, stat. Somebody cut away that shirt so we can assess the arms, neck, chest." The smaller woman barked commands. With a touch of the surreal Lori realized that this was the team who had nearly delivered Mikayla.

Now here they were again, reaching out to save a life instead of welcoming one into the world. Following the man who cradled Tyler in his arms, she kept up her prayers for everyone involved. Now her prayers had words again, blessings for Kenny and Rosa as they worked over Mike, for the nameless man who was giving her son oxygen, for all the people milling around here beginning to put out the fire and treat the people involved.

Looking back she could hear Dogg, still barking his lungs out under the tree. Beside him Gloria stood, white as the blanket around her shoulders, holding Mikayla and watching as Kenny and Rosa labored over her son.

They had so much in common at this moment. From across the yard, Lori prayed fervently. *Please, Lord, don't let either of us lose our sons.* It was all she could do for now. Catching Gloria's gaze across the space, she clasped her hands. Gloria saw the gesture and nodded, sinking down beside Dogg. Lori could see her lips moving, as well. Gloria had one arm around the baby, the other hand in the big animal's fur. Dogg lay down next to her and stopped barking while around them all the chaos of the fire filled the yard.

Chapter Fifteen

Mike opened his eyes and knew exactly where he was. He wasn't happy with that knowledge, but he recognized the look and the smell of a hospital even before he could figure out why he was there. In a few moments that became clear, as well.

He was foggy, probably from drugs. If he'd sucked in as much smoke in that house as he expected he had, life wasn't going to be pleasant for a couple of days. He couldn't remember much after staggering out of the house with Tyler. Fresh air had never felt so good. Then Kenny and Rosa and others had swarmed over him and things got kind of hazy after that.

Time to try and take some kind of assessment of what was what. There was definitely an oxygen mask over his face, but no breathing tube. That was a good sign. It was the worst smoke inhalation that he'd ever had to deal with, but the lack of a breathing tube, or a hole in his throat, were very good signs.

His right arm hurt worse than he could ever describe. He vaguely remembered thrusting it out on the charge out of Tyler's bedroom, keeping a falling piece of ceiling from hitting the boy. Obviously the burning chunk hit him instead. The good news, he told himself, was that if his arm hurt this severely, it was a second-degree burn. Third-degree burns destroyed enough tissue and nerve endings that it didn't hurt as badly. The pain was saved for later, for the skin grafts.

This was bizarre. He was almost thinking like Lori might, trying to find the little miracles in this awful situation. Was that a consequence of starting to trust God like she did? He'd have to ask her, when he could talk. And when he could talk to her. Where was she?

There was nobody else in this hospital room, a fact that surprised him. Once he knew where he was, he expected a few people around him, from nurses and doctors to his mom and Lori.

Of course the women wouldn't be here if they were in another hospital instead. A thrill of fear coursed through him at the thought of Lori standing over another bed like this, watching Tyler. *Please, God, let him be okay. I can take the pain. But let him be okay.* It was the last of his coherent thoughts before he drifted off in his haze of drugs and pain to where the nightmares waited.

Hours later, or perhaps only moments that felt like hours, he swam to the surface again. This time the room was full of people, as he'd expected. A nurse was changing an intravenous bag, there was at least one other medical person helping her do stuff and Gloria, looking frazzled, stood in the corner watching everything. He wanted to tell her he was all right. But even if he spoke behind this oxygen mask, she wouldn't be able to understand him.

No one would for a couple of days, Mike suspected. His throat felt raw, as if he was suffering from a bad case of strep throat. If he had a voice at this point, it wouldn't be pretty.

The nurse was the first one to notice that his eyes were open. ''Hey, Mrs. Martin, he's with us. Come over here and talk to him while I mess around with this. Maybe you can distract him from the nasty things I have to do. Just move in on that left side and you'll be okay. You can touch anything over there and not cause him any pain.''

Any more pain, Mike felt like telling her. Like he'd notice much more anyway. The drugs seemed to be doing their job as best they could, but to cause him more pain than he was already in, someone would have to rip off body parts. And even the burn nurses wouldn't start doing that for another day or two.

His mother was there in front of him. "Do you know where you are?"

"Hospital," he mouthed, hoping he could make himself understood. "Which one?" he rasped. It didn't look like the Peace Hospital in town that he was familiar with. And he knew about most departments there from visiting other people or getting them to the place.

"This is the burn unit at St. John's in Washington. It was the closest place that had everything you needed." Her voice was a bit shaky. Mike wanted to reach out and hold on to her, tell her everything was going to be okay. It was rough to see his mom this worried.

"Tyler? Lori and the baby?" he mouthed. He hoped his mom could understand that part. It weighed on his mind heavier than his own burns to know that Tyler was all right. If the boy was as uninjured as possible, he could take the next few days like a man, knowing he'd done his job.

"Tyler?" His mother asked, and he nodded as best he could. "He's here, but not for long probably. They're going to keep him overnight, treat him for smoke inhalation and make sure he's okay. But he has no burns, and he's already trying to fight his way out of bed so he can come see you.''

That was Tyler. Mike felt relief that the boy was basically all right. ''And I'll have you know that he insisted on having that toy fire engine ride here in the ambulance with him. Last I looked it was on the bedside table, because that was the closest the nurses would let him have it. If it was up to him, it would be in the bed.''

Mike smiled. Anything that was happening right now was bearable knowing Tyler was all right, and Lori and the baby stayed safe. There was something else he wanted to tell his mother, or ask her. Whatever it was, he couldn't form the words. It would come back later, he was sure of it. ''I love you,'' he mouthed to her. Reaching for her hand, he squeezed it.

''Oh, Mike, I love you, too. I was so worried. I still am, but I know you're going to be all right now. It may be a rough couple of days, but we should be able to put up with that. We have before.''

He tried to nod to agree with her. It took a lot of energy, and that was something he didn't seem to have much of. He was drifting off again. The nurse was still doing something that didn't feel too good. And now he remembered what he wanted to ask her. He needed something for the nightmares or flashbacks he was having. He didn't remember them from other fire-and-rescue episodes, but they were there now whenever he closed his eyes. *Okay, Lord. Time to help me ride out another wave of this stuff.* If he couldn't get any medication that would quench his fear, prayer would work. If Lori were here, she'd tell him that it would work better than any other medicine. He smiled, thinking of her and that piece of wisdom. The noise in the room receded as Mike drifted off again, back to the place where everything was on fire….

Had she ever been this tired before? Lori thought not. Even that second day after Mikayla was born, when she felt as if she'd walked face first into a brick wall, there hadn't been this kind of exhaustion.

Everything she owned was probably gone. She couldn't imagine what kind of effort it was going to take to go through things in that house and find anything worth saving. She praised God again that Tyler was not badly hurt and she and the baby were both untouched. At least they were untouched physically. But her heart hurt.

What was the purpose of all this? Why did the Martins have to lose part of their property? Mike was lying in a bed in this same hospital in far worse shape than Tyler was. And to what end? The only good, if you could call it that, which might come out of this would ultimately ruin another family's life. Clyde Hughes wasn't an island any more than anyone else, and his actions would rebound on his wife and children.

"Mom? I don't feel so good again," Tyler croaked from the bed.

"Ring the button on the bed. Let me get the bucket," Lori said, used to this by now. The doctors and nurses had warned her that nausea and vomiting were one way the body cleansed itself of the smoke for hours, or even days, after exposure. And, thank heavens, the staff psychologist also explained that just dealing with the fear that was left over from the fire could make Tyler feel ill, as well.

So it wasn't a surprise to deal with these bouts every couple of hours. Lori prayed that they'd subside soon. Tyler was sick again, but he'd pushed the call button this time. It was taped to the rail of the bed, where he could have control of it. The doctors said that was important, too, to give him as much control as possible over life in the hospital.

The only thing he had absolutely no control over was sharing his room with his mother. She wasn't going anywhere for quite some time, except perhaps to look in on Mike.

Even with all there was to do for Tyler, Lori's arms felt empty without the baby. She was so thankful that Carrie had found a way for Tyler's preschool teacher to take Mikayla in for a few days. There was just nobody else right now; Gloria was at the hospital, as well, and Lori knew that even if she called what little of her family remained, no one would come to Friedens to help her out of trouble. They'd pretty much cut ties when they found out Gary had gone to jail, and nothing had ever restored the relationship.

So here she was, pretty much alone. No, never totally alone, she reminded herself as the nurse bustled in to help with Tyler. God was here with her, even in this awful situation. And He'd stay here by her side no matter what happened. Still, while the nurse was getting Tyler set to rights, and talking about a Popsicle for him to replace some of his lost fluids, Lori wished she could travel a different road for a while. One that still led her to walk with the Lord, but maybe through a shallower valley. Or even a nice, sunny meadow. She smiled a little at the thought. There was definitely a meadow someplace in her future. All she had to do was find it.

The nightmare was the worst yet. Mike actually yelled as he came into consciousness. It hurt like blazes. There was a cool, comforting hand on his forehead when he opened his eyes. Lori. She looked like a vision. "Are you real?"

"Ouch. Don't talk. Yes, of course I'm real, silly. Your mom needed a break and Tyler is sound asleep. I'm wearing a beeper so the nurses' station can get in touch with me if he wakes up. I couldn't stay away any longer."

He slipped off the oxygen mask, earning himself a glare. "I can do this once in a while. I'll probably be off it tomorrow anyway." Even whispering didn't feel so great, but he had to talk. "He's okay, right?"

"Tyler? A lot better than you. Mike, I can't ever thank you enough for this." Her eyes were brimming.

"Don't try. I owe you as much as you owe me."

Lori's brow crinkled. "How can that be? All you've done is take care of me since we met."

"Yes, but you brought something with you I didn't have before. Faith. Lori, I didn't go into that fire alone."

He didn't say any more, but she understood. "Oh, Mike, that's great. I wish I could do something for you to ease the hurt. I've been praying all the time. If there's any silver lining to this, maybe this is it."

She never ceased to amaze him. The woman had lost just about everything she owned. Her son was in the hospital. And she was rejoicing with him, actually rejoicing over his newfound faith. "If you want to pray about something, ask the Lord to take away these nightmares. Or visions. Or whatever they are.''

''Bad, huh?'' She stroked his forehead again.

''The worst.'' He started to tell her about them, but she put those soft, blessedly sweet fingertips on his lips and he kissed them instead of talking.

''Don't tell me. Not in words. How about I get you a pad and pencil and you can write them down?'' Then she looked him over and grimaced. ''Guess that would be pretty hard to do without putting a lot of strain on that right arm.''

He shrugged, mostly on the left side. It hurt less that way. ''I'm supposed to keep things flexible. We could try.''

''Then I'll go find something. Tyler's been drawing pictures himself. Big ugly ones with lots of orange and red crayon. Maybe I'll get you a box of crayons, too.''

''Might help,'' he said. He smiled at her, and she leaned over him, dropping a soft kiss on his lips, then settling the oxygen mask back in place.

''You're not done with that thing yet,'' she told him, sounding stern. ''And I want you without it as soon as possible. Your mom should be back soon. We were going to meet up in the chapel at two, then go home.''

He raised his eyebrows in a question. "Two?" he asked behind the oxygen mask.

"Yes, it's the middle of the night. Now try and get some sleep and I'll send your mom up. God bless, Mike." She smoothed his hair and left the room, leaving him to silently wish God's blessing on her, as well, as he drifted off again. Maybe this time it would be a peaceful sleep.

The chapel was small, and at this time of night it was silent. A soft glow lit it, from candles in the front and soft lights in the ceiling. Lori entered from the back, finding Gloria in the second pew. She sat, slumped a little, and Lori's heart went out to her. Gloria looked older and more frail than she had ever seemed before.

Slipping into the pew with her, she prayed silently for a moment. She was still getting a strong urge to bring up a subject that she could never take back once it was broached. *Please, can't we just skip this?* she asked God, knowing in advance what His answer would be.

Nobody else knew what was dragging Gloria down to the depths of despair. They had nearly lost their sons together, and it forged a bond that wouldn't be broken by any of life's questions, no matter how tough. Lori took a deep breath, weighing her words.

"Well, my beeper hasn't gone off. That's a blessing, because it means that Tyler is sleeping peacefully. Mike isn't, though. He's having some awful nightmares or flashbacks."

"Did he ever tell you about the other fire?" Gloria leaned against the back of the bench. "He wasn't much older than Tyler."

"No. Could that be where his nightmares are coming from?"

"Maybe. He was helping his dad rake and burn leaves. John left him alone for a while, and Mike got very interested in those burning leaves. Next thing we knew the garage was on fire. John rushed in there to try and save the car, or at least get the gas can and the mower out of there before they exploded and caused an even worse blaze. Mike was panic-stricken. I had to hold him physically to keep him from following his dad in there."

"It must have been awful."

"It was. The worst of it was that about four days later was when John had his last heart attack. Mike didn't know about the earlier ones... What do you tell a six-year-old boy? It took years to convince him that he hadn't killed his daddy somehow by setting the garage on fire."

"Good heavens. No wonder going into the fire has given him nightmares. And I thought it was something else altogether." Lori felt washed in gratitude that she hadn't said anything about her other suspicions.

"Oh, you're right about that, too." Gloria's blue eyes were frank and unclouded. "His fascination with fire when he was six was a leftover from another life. We could never find out what had happened. But he had experiences before he was ever my son that drew him to fire."

"So he *is* adopted?"

Gloria nodded. "How did you know? No one in Friedens has any idea that Mike is adopted. He doesn't know himself."

"Intuition. Gut feelings. I have no idea." Lori's head was spinning. "You're going to have to tell him, you know."

Gloria slumped against the seat. "You're right. I'm going to break a twenty-five-year-old promise to a dead man when I do it, but you are so right. How do I find the strength? And what will it do to my life?"

"I can't imagine. Why don't we sit here together and pray about it. Surely if anybody can tell you what words to use, it has to be the Lord."

Gloria still looked ahead, but she reached out a hand to Lori. "I've never prayed out loud with anybody like that. But yes, it would be a good idea now. Help me find the right words."

Feeling the older woman's hand trembling, Lori

grasped it and began with her. "We're here in your presence, Lord, looking for healing. Physical healing for Mike and Tyler, and healing of the soul…" The little chapel felt like a place of miracles now in the middle of the night. Not just little miracles, but great big ones with wings.

Chapter Sixteen

Tyler's room was crowded. The nurse was going through last-minute checks to make sure he was truly ready to be discharged. Lori jiggled Mikayla, who seemed happy to be back in her mother's arms. She was contentedly sucking on one fist. And Hank Collins paced in front of her, scowling.

"There is just no other choice, young lady. You're going to have to say yes to our offer of protective custody, at least until the grand jury gets done with all this."

"Where? And how?" Lori challenged. "I've already shifted these children around twice in as many months. How do we handle things this time?"

Hank stopped pacing and folded his arms. "Gloria and I have worked things out. I can't tell you here and now where you're going. If I did, it wouldn't be protective custody.'' Lori was ready to tell him that hospital nurses weren't likely to be working for Hughes, or a drug syndicate. However, Hank wasn't going to take the argument so she just listened.

He stopped pacing. "Rest assured nobody's going to find you right away. And that's important when you're the main evidence we have on somebody as determined as Hughes."

"Why did he do it? I still can't imagine him throwing away everything he owns this way."

"Crazily enough, he did it for the best reason you can imagine—love." Hank shook his head. "He sent his little girl away to college and she did a whole lot of partying. Rehab didn't help, and he didn't want her getting street drugs from just anywhere."

The thought sickened Lori. The man would supply his own child with drugs? It gave her chills. Hank read the horror on her face. "I know. It doesn't make sense to me, either. I've got kids and I'd cut off my arm, or one of theirs, before I'd let them use anything illegal with my knowledge. But it made sense somehow to him. And he was bound and determined to keep things going. By the end, even setting fire to your house to destroy the evidence made sense.''

It numbed her mind. Lori was past imagining all of this. "So you think that somebody might try to get to us again? We really need to hide out?''

"It's not hiding out, exactly. This would be a perfectly comfortable place. It just wouldn't be Gloria's house, like you expected." Hank looked around the room. "And I'm not saying any more here. Except that you're leaving here in a squad car and you're going where I take you. Got that?''

Lori sighed. "Got it. Will you be this tough on Gloria if you guys get married, Hank?''

The sheriff blushed. "Probably not. She can wrap me around her little finger worse than my baby Carrie can. But don't tell her that.''

Lori felt a giggle ready to escape. "I won't. Yet. But in trade we're going to do a little negotiating on this safe house thing.''

"Why am I not surprised?" Hank sighed in resignation. "Let me carry some of this stuff so we can get out of here before I've negotiated myself into a corner.''

The next time Mike woke up in daylight there was a stack of yellow legal pads and a couple of sharpened pencils on his bedside table. And next to them, just so he'd know where they came from, was a box of crayons. He smiled seeing it all, and promptly put the top legal pad to use.

Writing wasn't easy. But he felt so much better with the fire demons on paper instead of just haunting him from inside. Some of the dreams or nightmares he could understand.

Those weren't the ones that woke him in a cold sweat. He didn't like dreaming that he was in Tyler's room, it was on fire again and it had no door. But he could understand where the vision came from.

It was the same with the one with his father yelling at him in front of a burning garage. Not that his dad had yelled when he burned down his garage, or even when he'd charged out after removing the most explosive materials. Mike had been sure as a six-year-old that his dad should have yelled. That maybe if he had, that fatal heart attack wouldn't have claimed him. When he spent long evenings watching his mother work at home after a long day at Martin Properties, he was sure as a grade-schooler that all their problems were his fault. So those scenes were understandable, as well. They almost made him feel better.

No, it was the scenes of the trailer, dilapidated like Lori's, maybe even worse, swamped in flames that mystified him. Where did those come from? Why was he reliving scenes of absolute terror running through a trailer? And there was the cage, too. Those were the worst. Those were the ones he wrote down several times.

Even telling it on paper made his forehead sweat cold droplets. He was peering through wire mesh, taller than he was. His hands clasped the mesh and on the other side was the sound of fire, the smell of smoke. And danger. Yet every muscle in his body urged him to climb that barrier and go back to the other side where the fire roared. He wanted to run to it. He could hear voices screaming, telling him not to move. He wanted to run so much. But the voices were telling him to stay put. And that was the scene that woke him up, playing behind his eyelids in a nightmare dance.

That one didn't disappear once he wrote it down. He felt better, as if there were fewer gargoyles hunkered down on his chest, but the weight wasn't gone. After a while he even got out Lori's crayons and used a clean sheet on the legal pad. The crossed pattern of the cage mesh reminded him of something else, but he couldn't figure out what. Coloring in the inferno behind the mesh, he began to understand why Tyler used this method of expressing himself. For things one lacked words for, color said a variety of things. After a few moments he could barely stand to touch the red and scarlet crayons.

There were patches of silver where the skin of

the trailer hadn't burned yet, and deep blue night sky. This was all so real, somehow, but so foreign to anything he had ever really seen before. A half hour of writing and drawing went by in a flash. Putting down the pad he felt cleansed. His pain medication was wearing off, and he was feeling the effects of his first morning without supplemental oxygen. But after using Tyler and Lori's crayons, he felt like he could take a nap without waking to horror from within.

When he woke, his mother was sitting in the bedside chair. She had apparently been reading what he'd written, looking at what he'd drawn. And she had been crying. Mike couldn't remember seeing her so obviously disturbed since shortly after his father's death.

"Hey," he called softly, reaching out his good hand. "It isn't that bad. I'm gonna live, Mom."

She took a deep breath and opened her eyes wide. "I know. I'm not worried about that anymore. Now I have to admit I probably aged a decade watching those paramedics working on you outside the house. But I'm pretty sure you're going to get through this with nothing worse than a pucker on one arm where that delightful skin graft is going to be."

"Yeah, I'm looking forward to that one myself. At least the area they can harvest from is huge. I've only got the one place bad enough to graft. That, as Lori would say, is one of life's little miracles.''

His mother shook her head. ''Those miracles. Where would we be if she hadn't come into our lives? If you hadn't brought her in, Mike?''

''You have this look on your face that says we'd be better off in some ways if I hadn't.'' His mother grimaced a little, as she did when he was right and she didn't want him to be. ''But honestly, I think it was God's doing, Lori and Tyler and Mikayla coming into our lives.''

''You're probably right. It's just that if they hadn't I wouldn't be sitting in this hospital trying to find the strength to do something I should have done more than twenty years ago.''

Now he was truly mystified. He was ready for his mother's regrets on Lori's presence in their lives—what mother ever thought a woman was good enough for her baby, even if she didn't cause trouble? But this was something different.

''Tell me what you mean.'' He grasped her hand tighter, and she squeezed back. Was she trembling?

''First, let me say that I have loved you with all my heart since the moment I first set eyes on you.''

''I know that. Doesn't every mother say that?'' he said softly.

''I expect so. But you weren't a few minutes old when I first saw you. You were two and a half.''

The room seemed to close down to a narrow tunnel, holding only the two of them. Mike could barely take in what his mother was telling him. Still, he nodded for her to continue, and she did, still gripping his hand so firmly that his fingers started turning white around the edges.

Her story went on, sometimes in long stretches, sometimes in bits she had to force out. "I didn't think it was such a good thing keeping it all from you," Gloria told him. Shortly after her first stunning pronouncement Mike had asked her to leave the room for a few moments, and against the advice of the burn nurses, he insisted on putting on the jeans and shirt that were in his small closet. He was not having the most important discussion of his life in one of those hospital gowns that opened in embarrassing places.

So now they sat in the two chairs in the room. He was still hooked up to an IV pole and other inconveniences, but he felt more like himself dressed and sitting up straight.

"How did you keep this big a secret? I mean, everything you did cannot be legal." Mike ran his good hand through his hair. "I've seen my birth certificate. It says you are my parents, that I was born in Missouri, the whole bit. How much of that is true?"

"You were born in Missouri. And by the time

we adopted you, you had no living parents. John wanted to make sure of that. When he found out we couldn't have our own children, it hit him hard. We hadn't married all that young, and by the time we knew we had to adopt if we were going to have a child, I was past thirty-five. He was fifty.''

"Why was it so important that I didn't have any other parents?"

"Have you ever heard of the orphan trains?"

Now where was this going? "Yeah, but isn't that Civil War stuff? What has it got to do with us?"

"Everything. Those orphan trains brought children to Missouri much later than the Civil War. They brought one little boy from New York in 1929 who was old enough to remember the mother who had to give him up. And who never really did get a new family, just drifting from one foster situation to the other.''

"Dad?" This went a long way toward explaining this whole confusing mess.

"Yes. They even changed his name. He had been Erich Steinmetz in New York. In Missouri he was John Martin. The Martin part came from the second foster family, who almost adopted him. He always said no child of his would go through what he did as a child.''

"It's going to take me a while to handle all this.''

"I'm sure. We did it out of love, Mike. You have to realize that."

He got out of his chair and put his arms around his mother, no matter how much it pulled and hurt on his arm. "I know that. I could never doubt that. But it sure raises a lot of questions. Do you know anything about my life before I came to you?"

"Some. Not a lot. There was some hardship involved and the state thought it best if you knew as little as possible. Then your father—I guess I should just say John—" She faltered.

"No. My father. I never knew any other."

"All right. Your father found a lawyer who would not only handle the adoption, but also for an extra fee handle a second set of paperwork that gave you a new birth certificate and other things that proved you were ours all along. I wasn't so sure about that part, but John said it had to be that way. After that last heart attack he made me promise that I'd never tell you anything different."

"Last heart attack? There had been more?"

"Several. He knew by the time you were four or five that it was a matter of time. That's why he was adamant about not telling you. He was sure you'd have enough problems to deal with without another one."

"Maybe he was right. Maybe not. Whatever the case, it's in God's hands now. Surely He wouldn't have brought me this far to let me handle something like this alone now.''

Gloria seemed surprised by his response. ''You don't hate me?''

He let go of her hands, and sat back in his chair. ''Mom, how could I hate you? I just need time to figure this all out.''

''We have all the time in the world now that it's out in the open,'' Gloria said.

There was a knock on the door. ''We're sneaking in,'' Lori said softly. ''As much as you can sneak with this big a contingent.''

She slipped into the room, Mikayla in her arms. She looked wonderful to Mike, and the baby, noisily slurping one fist, was a picture. Tyler followed them into the room, carrying his ever-present fire engine.

''Hey, Mike. Can I hug you? Mom said I had to ask.''

''You can, but put that big old metal thing down on the bed first, Ty. Get up here on this side of my lap and let me look at you.'' Tyler did what he was told and Mike looked him over. ''Looking good, bud. You going home?''

''Yeah, sort of. Mom says we're leaving the hospital, but we're not going to your house.'' His expression said what Tyler thought of that.

Gloria looked up at that remark. ''What? I don't

get my goat helper back? Hank, that is not what we talked about.''

Mike hadn't noticed that Hank made up the tail of the parade until now. "Sorry, Gloria. There's no choice until the grand jury convenes.''

Lori was next to him now. "Hank insists that we're going to a safe house. I think it's an awful idea, but he's not letting me argue.''

Mike snorted. "Good. Anybody stupid enough to do…what was done the other night…'' He softened his words, thinking of the boy on his lap. "We will know where you are, won't we?''

Hank shook his head. "Not really. That's why I let her come by here, Mike. I can't have the whole county privy to what's going on. Then it wouldn't be a safe house, now would it?''

Mike started to protest, but looked at his mother. How would Hank Collins arrange a safe house without the help of the biggest property-management firm in the county? He raised an eyebrow silently and looked directly at Gloria. She gave him an enigmatic smile back. "All right. I'll leave it there. But this place has a phone, doesn't it?''

"Yes, it has a phone. Or at least I'll have a cell phone you can call that I'll carry with me. And I'll have a computer there so I won't let Martin Properties get further behind than they are already. It won't be forever. Hank says if things work out he'll let me have a police escort to the office and pre-school real soon.''

Lori leaned down and rested her head on top of his. The move brought Mikayla down to hair-grabbing level. There wasn't much damage she could do on Mike, but she tried. Those tiny fingers running through his hair were sweet.

"I guess we let Hank have his way, then. Thanks for telling me up front.''

Lori looked in his eyes, serious now. "You've had enough surprises for one day. I'm not adding one more.''

"So you knew about this?''

"I had an idea. I'm not sure how.''

"Yes, you are. You figured out the first time you left us alone how miserable I am with babies,'' Gloria said, laughing a little. "It's hard to hide.''

Tyler looked around at the adults. "What is everybody talking about? I want to go have lunch.'' He slid off Mike's lap and started looking at things on the bedside table. "Hey, Mom, Mike uses his crayons, too. Can we trade pictures? I drawed one of the fire, too. But yours is better.''

Mike felt his chest tighten. "Sure. We can swap if you want. Where's yours?''

"Here on the bed. I'll leave it with my fire engine. I don't need it anymore, and Mom says they have to fix your arm where you got burned.''

"Yeah, they do." His throat was tightening along with his chest. Mike promised himself that he would not tear up over this beautiful child and his generosity.

"Well, it really helped when they did the gross stuff to me if I had that fire engine to hold on to. I figure you can use it when they fix your arm. Then you can give it back to me. All right?" He laid his small hand on Mike's good arm.

"All right." The tears threatened anyway. This was a gift from God more precious than anything else he'd been given today. Or maybe ever. "And I'll be sure to give it back as soon as I can. Probably by Wednesday. Now give me another hug and let your mom hug me, too."

"Great," Tyler said, rolling his eyes. "More of that stuff. Are you going to kiss her, too?"

"You bet. Close your eyes if it bothers you." Mike felt a laugh replacing the tightness in his chest. Maybe, just maybe, the cage dreams would fade now.

Chapter Seventeen

It felt odd to go to the apartment in Union, knowing Mike was out of the hospital and back home. Lori thought maybe time would make things easier, but it didn't. A week after moving into the apartment everybody was still unsettled and grouchy.

Lori had her police escort now and was showing up at the office. Tyler loved riding a police car back and forth to preschool. Lori wasn't so sure she exactly adored having a uniformed officer pick her up every place. And it certainly didn't make Mike happy.

"This is driving me nuts, you know." Mike was scowling again. It was his favorite expression since he'd come back to work. Lori tried to humor him whenever possible. This kind of life wasn't doing her any good, either. The apartment in Union was nice, but it wasn't convenient. She missed being across the yard from Mike and his mom. It was aggravating having only a cell phone and a strangely rigged line for a modem so she couldn't even pick up the telephone and chat. And Union was just far enough that the hand-held radio, which somehow avoided being burnt to a crisp, was out of its three-mile range from the Martins.

So she felt isolated, which she knew wasn't the point of being in the apartment. Hank and his deputies checked on her daily, so she wasn't totally alone. And she was never out of the necessities like bread and milk because they didn't want her in the convenience stores closest to the place, so whoever was checking up on her always got "orders" and brought things to her.

Still, the distance brought up how much she and even the kids had gotten used to having Mike in and out of their life at will. Tyler missed piggyback rides and Miss Gloria's goats. Mikayla, who now recognized a variety of voices, seemed to be listening for Mike's even when she wasn't at work with her mother.

So Lori knew why Mike was unsettled and crabby. The distance, on top of his itching, healing skin grafts and everything else had to be aggravating. "I know this has to be hard on you, too. I keep hoping Hank will tell me the grand jury has convened and we can get back to a normal life. Although I don't know what that would mean, besides a real phone line.''

That brought on another scowl from Mike. ''Oh, come on. It would mean a lot more changes. You'd move back with us, wouldn't you? At least for as long as there's an us to move back to. I keep waiting for those two to announce an engagement I am not even supposed to know about. Then I figure I'll be house hunting, too.''

''Your mother would never kick you out of your own apartment.''

''I know she wouldn't. But if you think I'm living with a pair of middle-aged newlyweds *and* a herd of goats on the same property without your comforting presence, you have another think coming.''

That did it. She had to laugh. ''Hey, aren't you doing your Bible study like you promised? Remember Philippians 4? 'I can do all things in Christ which strengthen me.'''

Mike smiled in response. ''Verse 13. But I don't think it applies to goats.''

''Oh, definitely to goats. There are lots of goats in the Bible.''

''Not floppy-eared Nubian ones with odd dispositions. One of those stinkers got out of her compound the other day and I had to chase it out of your house. She was eating what was left of the artificial flowers in the kitchen.''

Lori found herself giggling. She couldn't resist. "Oh, great. Those pink ones? That was one of the few things I really wanted to save. And a goat ate it.''

Mike shook his head. "How can you laugh about that?''

Lori shrugged. "Better to laugh, I guess. How about if after work I take everybody, go back to the house and sift through stuff while it's still light. Tyler can help your mom feed her awful goats, and you can come with us and jiggle Mikayla while I go through drawers.''

Mike perked up a little. "Sounds good. Then I can take everybody out for burgers afterward, and take you home....''

"You can take us out for burgers," she said, laying her fingers on his mouth to stop the rest of his sentence. It was a mistake to touch him like that, even in the middle of the office. His lips were warm velvet under her fingers. She lost the thread of what she was going to say while she concentrated on the delightful feel of him. "Where was I going with this? Oh, yes. You can take us out for burgers. But you can't take us home. You know that. We'll go home via my police taxi service, as usual.''

His lips crinkled in a frown under her fingers and she moved them to let him talk. ''I really thought that losing that heap of junk you were driving would be a blessing. That you'd at least need me for my car, if nothing else.''

''I need you for dozens of things, Mike. The car isn't really one of them. Now kiss me quickly while there's nobody walking by the window. That's something I definitely need you for.''

His answering kiss wasn't as quick as Lori had suggested. But it felt wonderful, and she couldn't complain. How would it sound anyway, to tell Mike that he was kissing her for too long? The gleam in his eyes when he pulled away told her he already knew what she would have said. He walked back to his desk slowly. And when he got there, he turned and winked. It was going to be a long time until two when they could all pack up and leave the office.

''Are you nervous?'' Lori looked more than nervous; she looked like she was ready to jump out of her skin.

''Terrified. Keep holding my hand.'' Her eyes were huge as they stood in the hallway of the county courthouse, waiting for her to be called in to testify before the grand jury.

Even though they'd waited for this moment for weeks, Mike wanted to take it back. Lori was a wreck. "I won't let go," he promised. "Not until you have to go in there where I can't go. Want to pray about the whole thing some more?"

Lori nodded. "Yes. Definitely. You would do that with me?"

"For you, anything. And that's a big anything. I'm still working on this prayer stuff, especially with anybody else around to hear me."

They found a bench close to the door where Lori would be called in. No one in the courthouse hall seemed to notice them as they settled there. Mike prayed softly, but still out loud. He asked for God's guidance in the situation, for His peace to be with Lori as she did what was right.

"Amen," Lori chimed after him. She squeezed both his hands, reminding him how much smaller her fingers were than his.

"Hey, once this is over, can I finally drive you home?"

"It's probably still against Hank's rules, but I'm going to say yes," Lori told him. "I feel like this is a big day. Closing one chapter in my life, and opening up another one. We should celebrate that somehow."

"I plan on celebrating several different ways." Mike felt very tongue-tied suddenly. This was the opening he'd been waiting for, and now he felt reserved and shy. He'd just asked for God's guidance for Lori. Surely he could claim it for himself, as well, couldn't he? He breathed a silent prayer and let out a deep breath.

"This new chapter stuff. Does it mean that you feel at peace with Gary now?"

Lori looked surprised. "I think I already do. I'm not doing this for him, Mike. If I'm doing it for anybody, it's for my children. Some day they'll be old enough to ask about their father. I won't keep any secrets from them. We've both seen what that can do."

"And how." Mike shook his head at the vision of his mom in family therapy with him after his skin grafts. Some of it had been as painful as the burn healing, but all of it had been necessary. They were making progress toward a new relationship, based on honesty.

He still didn't know as much as he'd like about the life he had before he came to the Martins. He probably never would. The information was spotty at best, and much had been destroyed by the lawyer's misguided attempt to create his new identity.

Still, he was looking ahead. Mike was getting to know this person who lived inside his skin. He was a different person than he'd been before the fire, and it took some getting used to. "You're right in keeping as few secrets as possible from them. It may be years, decades even, before they want to know everything."

"But when they do, I want to tell them I did what I could for their father's memory. That he was, in the end, a good man who made some big mistakes. And one of those mistakes cost him his life." Her eyes misted with tears and Mike reached up, swiping a thumb across her soft cheek. "I'm not sure if it matters in the end if Hughes gave him the drugs that made him run off the road, or just had someone else do it. Either way, we'll probably never get a confession. But at least we know something."

"You're a good woman. But then I've said that since we first met."

"And I've said that being good doesn't matter." She laughed wryly through her tears. "Good hasn't helped me much in this situation. I'm not even sure, still, that I did the right thing."

Mike wanted to fold her in his arms and keep her safe. But this slender body that felt so good in front of him held a tiger's spirit, and held too tightly, she would scratch. He had to learn to let her fight her own battles, even when it worried him. "You did what you thought was right. And you're doing it now." The door next to them opened and a bailiff stepped out.

"Loretta Christine Harper."

Mike couldn't help himself. *"Loretta Christine?"*

She frowned a mock frown. "Not one word, mister. That is what it says on my driver's license. Just sit here and pray for me the entire time that I'm in there. Got it?"

"Got it. Loretta." Oh, there was a bit of fun to be had with this one, Mike was sure. Lori stood up, ran damp hands down her tailored black pants and walked into the chambers with the bailiff who had called her name.

Hey, Lord. What's this Loretta business about? No matter what I'm supposed to call her, be with her in there.

Mike couldn't sit on the bench while she was in there. It felt better pacing. So he paced, for over an hour until Lori came out. And then he held her while she cried for a while, which she assured him was due to tears of relief. He wasn't sure if that was all she was feeling, but he held her and let her cry. And then he took her home.

Her apartment in Union was nice. It wasn't as convenient as the green house, of course, but knowing that his mother arranged it from one of their good rental properties, Mike knew it was nice.

"Now, aren't you proud of me for not checking this out earlier?" Mike asked as he parked in front of the building. "I could have done that, you know. I mean, it's only a process of elimination on how many properties we deal with over here."

"But you were a good, honest person and did what you were supposed to." Lori leaned over and hugged him before she got out of the car. "I know how hard that was for you, and I really respect you for doing it. But at the same time I'm really glad that you can know where I am now."

"That makes two of us." Mike got out of the car and followed her up the stairs to her door. "You're going to have to start letting me act like a gentleman, though. I haven't opened a door for you in ages."

"And you probably won't unless I'm carrying Mikayla." Lori unlocked the door and called into the apartment, "We're home. I brought Mike with me. Or if you want to get really picky, he brought me."

"Good." Gloria came out from the kitchen. "I got spaghetti sauce going so you don't have to cook. And we can't really stay and have it with you, because I left a batch in the slow cooker at home. Kayla's asleep, thank heavens. This time she and I seemed to get along better.''

''Of course. She's getting to be more fun every day, isn't she?''

Gloria nodded. ''I love the noises she makes. She has this brilliant look, like she wants to just open her mouth and start a real conversation.''

''She gets that from her mother,'' Mike quipped, earning himself a poke in the ribs. ''Oof. Think we should go home, Mom?''

''Not yet. I want to hear how everything went. And I have to give Lori her messages. Between here and the office, relaying phone calls gets complicated.''

''I'll say. I'm glad that won't have to last much longer,'' Lori said. ''Let me fill you in on what I can, and you can give me my messages. Although I can't imagine that any of them are terribly important or you would have taken care of them at work for me.''

''I did, when I got in there this morning. All of them that I could,'' Gloria said. ''There was one that wasn't related to work, from a man who left a number. He said his name was Carl Brenner and he needed to talk to you as soon as possible.''

Although the name meant nothing to his mother, Mike could see it meant something to Lori. She turned pale, standing still for a moment, then seemed to shake things off just as quickly. "Great. I'll call him back when I can. Let me get us both something to drink while we talk. That grand jury stuff is thirsty work. And I know the baby will want to eat the moment she wakes up. So if I'm going to put my feet up and have a cold drink, it better be soon."

Mike wished Tyler had been home. That would have given him something to do while the women talked. As it was, he felt like a third wheel during the conversation. "When do we need to pick Tyler up from school?" he asked, pretty sure he knew the answer already.

"Not until four. He's staying with the day care kids just for today. Unless you want to go get him and bring him back for me. That would be wonderful," Lori said with a smile.

"I'll do it. If they'll let me pick him up."

"You and your mom are the only ones they'll release him to besides me. If anybody gives you any trouble, you can give them Tyler's password."

"I don't even have to ask what that is," Mike said. "It has to be fire engine."

"You know us way too well." Lori shook her head.

Not always, Mike thought, wondering who the strange man in Lori's life was that made her heart miss a beat just by the mention of his name in

conversation. Until today he would have said that
his name was the only one that could make her
falter like that. It bore thinking about.

A week later Mike was even more confused. Lori
came to work at the office every day now, instead
of doing most of her work from the apartment
where she could hide out. And she came to work
whistling and humming and went home that way.
But there seemed to be something contained, almost distant about her in an odd way.

The strangest part was that she was radiantly
happy. At first he thought that was just because the
weight of the grand jury testimony was off her
shoulders. When he brought that up, she seemed
glad that it was over, but not ecstatic. She and Gloria had several conversations behind closed doors,
which he wondered about.

The strangest thing was that his mother accepted
an invitation to dinner at Lori's apartment without
ever once suggesting that she cook at the house
instead, and have the Harpers over. That was so
odd that Mike had to remark on it, even though he
was invited along. For all the satisfaction he got
asking his mother questions about the whole event,
he might as well have talked to his computer
screen.

It wasn't about Hank and his mom. That much

he knew, because the older couple had "gone public" as they put it, and lunched together several times a week, even at the Town Hall. Everybody in Friedens probably knew they were an item by now.

This was something different, and Mike felt more clueless than usual. He finally just stopped arguing and wondering and agreed to drive his mother to the apartment on the designated night. Lori seemed as excited as Tyler might be, almost hugging herself with happiness.

Meanwhile, Mike worked through a few plans of his own, keeping much more silent about what he was doing than the women did. If he were going to be rejected, he would do it quietly. And if he was accepted after all his planning was done, he could be happy about it then. No sense in investing too much into things before they happened.

So Mike found himself driving his truck over to Union with Gloria in the passenger seat, dressed better than she had been for work that day. What was that about? And why did she insist that he wear a shirt and tie to dinner at Lori's? He was going to be a wreck by the time the kids got done with him.

They parked outside and Mike noticed at least one unfamiliar vehicle. A pickup truck much like his own, it wasn't one of the things he was used to seeing around the neighborhood. He'd gotten good at scouting out strange vehicles after all this mess with Hughes. "Hank could make me a deputy," he muttered under his breath.

"What?" his mother asked.

"Nothing." Better to just get to the door and find out what these two women had planned for him. He rang the outside bell and heard Tyler thunder down the hall.

"It's them, Mom. I can see Mike," he heard the boy call behind the door.

There was much more commotion behind the door. Behind him, Mike could hear his mother shifting nervously. They hadn't planned some kind of goofy surprise party, had they? His birthday wasn't for a month yet. Of course, that would make things much more surprising.

The door opened and Mike found himself facing a man he'd never seen before, but who looked oddly familiar. His dark hair was wavy, and his gray eyes wide. "Hi. I'm Carl Brenner. You don't know me yet."

Brenner. It was the name from Lori's message. What was this about? At first Mike felt hot under the collar, but then he paused. Lori wouldn't do anything to hurt him, so this had to be something unusual, but right. "Okay." Mike stood his ground, still wondering what this was about.

The man broke into tears right in front of him.

"This is crazy. I promised myself I would be cool. But I've been looking for you for twenty-five years." He came through the doorway, reaching for Mike. "I think—no, after seeing you, let me change that. I *know* I'm your brother."

Chapter Eighteen

"Tell him how this all worked out," Gloria urged Lori as they all settled in the living room of the apartment. She looked more animated than Lori expected. True, she seemed nervous. And she welcomed the interruptions the children caused during the evening. But she honestly seemed proud of all of this.

Nobody had eaten a lot of dinner. Lori wasn't surprised by that. She wasn't all that hungry herself, with the anticipation of everything traveling through her like butterfly wings. She was glad when they opted for conversation instead of dessert.

"Your mom really got me started on it. She suggested that since I was so good on the computer, I might try searching sites where people look for lost relatives.''

''And she found mine right away. That's what I mostly do for a living, or a calling, I guess you could say. Find people. Until this week, you're the only one I never had any success with.'' Carl was sitting on the apartment's battered couch, with Mike on the other end. To Lori they looked like bookends.

They were definitely a matched pair. Both handsome men, tall with similar features. What surprised Lori was that for two brothers who hadn't been raised together, their gestures and movements were similar. There were positions Carl took when sitting and speaking that looked just like Mike.

He was doing it now, using a sweeping hand gesture she'd seen dozens of times when Mike was on the phone trying to elaborate a point. ''Do you know what she sent me that convinced me? This woman faxed me a crayon drawing you had made in the hospital. I knew as soon as I saw it that you were my brother Danny.''

''You said that to me on the phone,'' Lori said. ''Explain it for us.''

Carl moved forward, and Mike leaned in to listen to him. They were, without a doubt, a fine-looking pair of men. That wasn't what made Lori's heart sing. It was the smile on Mike's face as he listened, the sparkle in his eyes that gave him a look of peace she'd never seen before.

"You couldn't really remember that. But you drew it. That's how we lost our parents, in that fire in the trailer where we all lived. You and I were the only ones who got out all right. I was terrified that you were going to bolt back in there."

"And you yelled at me to stay put. But I didn't want to."

Carl sat back, looking stunned. "Right. Do you remember that? How could you? You were only two."

"I don't remember it consciously. But after getting Tyler out of the fire I had all kinds of nightmares. Most of them faded in and out, but that one kept coming back. And it was so very real. It's good to know that it was real. Thanks for what you did, Carl."

Both men had a suspicious shine to their eyes. Lori was so choked up that she could barely hold back tears. She wasn't sure she wanted to keep them in much longer. Maybe it was the right thing to let them out.

It was Carl's response that started her weeping in earnest. "I've probably waited twenty-five years to hear you say those words. For so long, I concentrated on what I didn't do that day, and the days after. I got you out of the fire, Mike, but I wasn't able to stay with you. For years I felt like a failure because of that.''

Mike's brow wrinkled. ''How? You did get me out, and we lived. Carl, this little guy running around here is five. That's the age you said you were. Do you honestly think he would be capable of looking after a baby?''

Carl smiled, a rueful smile. ''No, not really. And I haven't felt that way in a while, either. Grace convinced me of that. You'll love my wife, Grace, and the kids. I can hardly wait to get together.''

''I'd like that, too.'' Mike looked over at Gloria. ''If that's okay with you, Mom. I can't tell you how excited I am to find a brother, to know what happened to me before. But no one could ever replace my mother.''

''I have no intention of doing that.'' Carl waved a hand, and Lori was struck by the elegance of the gesture, and the similarity to the way Mike did it. Did these two see how alike they were? ''I owe you the greatest debt, ma'am. Sometimes when I was a kid, the only thing that kept me sane was knowing that somewhere there were people who were very good to my brother. I am so happy to see that my dreams for him didn't even come close to the reality. I'd be honored if you could consider yourself part of our family somehow.''

Gloria was in worse shape than Lori was herself.

And that speech put her over the edge. Lori went over to the chair where Gloria sat and put an arm around her shoulders while she cried. The men looked at each other, both shifting uncomfortably in their seats.

"You handle this as well as I do, I see," Mike said. "I know you meant that in the best possible way. It's just that, well, they're women, aren't they?"

"And we do not speak the same language. Grace is always reminding me," Carl said. "She and her aunt, who is basically my mother-in-law, are always reminding me. So is my daughter, Maria. I guess I ought to say she's Grace's daughter, technically. She's only been mine since she was six, but I tend to forget that part. She's reached that magical age where she's part woman, part child and the looks I get sometimes…"

"Say no more. But if you have pictures of all these people, it might stop the waterworks," Mike said.

His mother looked up. "I hate to admit it, but he's right. And you're welcome, Carl. This is all so surprising to me, though. I was afraid that since we waited this long, somehow God was going to be angry with me for not letting Mike know sooner. That there would be no possible way that his first family would ever accept me or do anything but resent me.''

''And nothing could be farther from the truth,'' Lori said. ''Isn't that—''

''A miracle,'' Mike finished for her. They smiled across the room as Carl reached for his wallet and a stack of pictures inside.

''Speaking of miracles, let me show you our newest one,'' he said. ''His name is Daniel and yes, he was named for you. I promised Grace before he was born that our first child together would bear your name in some form. If he had been a girl, he would have been Danielle. I never forgot you.''

Lori went over to where Mike looked at the picture. ''Isn't this fantastic? You have two namesakes, Mike. One for each name. And both beautiful babies if I do say so myself.''

''You're allowed,'' Mike said. ''As the mother of one and the future aunt to the other, it makes perfect sense for you to admire them.''

''Future aunt?'' Carl quirked an eyebrow in a gesture that made Lori shiver, it was so like Mike. ''You didn't tell me that part on the phone.''

''Maybe because it's the first I've heard about it myself,'' Lori said, trying to keep her voice from shaking.

Mike looked over at his brother. ''I guess you got all the finesse in the family, huh? Somebody had to, because I'm hopeless. Shall I get down on one knee and make it official, Lori?''

She stood in front of him, fighting tears. Of all the things she expected tonight, this wasn't one of them. But it felt so right. ''No, please, don't. Where you are is just fine. If you really mean this, Mike…''

''I've never meant anything more. Lori Harper, you have been precious to me since the moment you walked into my life. You have filled empty spots in my heart I didn't even know *existed* before you came. Because of you I am a different person. Will you take that person into your heart? For good?''

''Forever.'' She couldn't hold the tears back. They trickled down her cheeks and she smiled, not bothering to wipe them away. Mike would do that for her soon enough. ''Are you sure you want a widow with two kids? And no money?''

''The money part doesn't bother me at all. What you've already given me is so much dearer than money. And that includes the opportunity to know your children. I can't imagine anything better than getting to live with them every day, unless it's getting to live with you.''

Lori didn't have enough strength in her knees to keep standing. Mike could see her shaking, and opened his arms. "Come on down here, girl. Want to start making some plans?"

"Yes. Yes, I believe I do, Mike." And she fell into his lap gratefully and kissed him, totally in awe of the way things were working out.

Epilogue

"I still think you're making a mistake," Tyler said, small fists bunched on his hips.

Lori looked past him into the crowded church. "I hope you don't mean about marrying Mike. Because I am going to do that, no matter what, Tyler." She couldn't imagine what had gotten into her son, now of all times.

He shook his head, rearranging the careful combing Gloria had done just moments previous, before Mike had escorted her up the aisle to her place as the mother of the groom, then gotten to the front of the church himself to wait. "No. I want you to marry Mike. That will make him my dad, and that's cool. I mean about the bear stuff. Dogg can growl. And I can, too. We could still be ring bears."

Lori leaned against the cool wall of the church, trying not to collapse in giggles. "No, Ty. You both really have to be ring bearers. Not bears. I know that you and Dogg are perfectly good at growling. But we don't need anybody to growl. We need you to carry the pillow with the rings on it."

Tyler rolled his eyes. "If you say so. I still think the other way sounds like more fun."

"I'm sure it does." Mike was going to love this one. She could hardly wait to tell him in a few moments—after the ceremony, when his laughter wouldn't confuse everyone in the church.

Down the red-carpeted aisle of the church, what looked like miles away, she could see him standing there, waiting for her. The organ was playing and Mike was just a little bit fidgety. Her man looked like he wanted to run one finger inside the collar of that white tuxedo shirt which fit so much tighter than the fire-and-rescue uniform he wore most days now.

She liked that uniform. If it had been up to her, she could have seen him married in it. But when she'd brought it up, he had told her he'd only agree if she wore one of the pantsuits she usually wore in her new management job with Martin Properties.

Lori declined the offer. She wanted a nice dress for her wedding. The soft pale pink she'd chosen felt good under her fingers as she touched the skirt. Dogg, standing next to Tyler, whined softly. "I know, you practiced this part and you know what to do. Time to go do it, both of you," she said, giving the big head a pat and sending him down the aisle with Tyler holding the totally unnecessary leash. Mike had insisted on Tyler being a ring bearer, and Lori had insisted on the big German shepherd. The two of them had done so much to bring the adults together. How could she deny either of them a place in this ceremony?

They made it down the aisle smoothly, and Tyler turned around briefly, giving her a "thumbs-up" sign, which made most of the churchgoers laugh.

"Okay, if they made it, that means it's your turn," Lori said to Carrie, who shone in her simple blue sheath.

"Let's just hope I make it down there that well, considering this is probably the first time I've worn heels since the senior prom," Carrie muttered.

"Remember, Philippians 4..."

"I know. I know. I can do anything through Christ who gives me strength. And falling on my face in front of a couple hundred people wouldn't do much for me, so I guess I can handle this." Carrie sighed and adjusted her flowers. She turned and took off down the aisle, with Lori praying for her.

That distracted her enough that she wasn't worried about her own trip. It wasn't the trip, exactly, that she was worried about anyway. Everybody here was a friend or relative somehow. She knew that in the front pew Carl's gorgeous wife, Grace, sat smiling, waiting for her, bouncing a baby on each knee. Daniel and Mikayla were good buddies for each other, and Kayla didn't fuss at all today when Lori had handed her off to "Aunt Grace."

If she had, one of Carl and Grace's two older kids would have made her smile anyway. Lori couldn't remember a time in her life when she had felt this surrounded by love and family.

"Okay, let's go," Hank whispered in her ear. "And I do appreciate the chance to do this. This way I'll be less nervous next month when the tables are turned and it's me up there, watching Mike walk his mother down the aisle."

"You'll have practice," Lori agreed. Hank looked fine in his tux, and she took his arm for the walk down the aisle. It only seemed to take a moment before she was there with Mike, and Hank was handing her off to this wonderful man.

"We made it," Mike said softly as the minister began the words of the service. "No falls, no distractions, no crying babies. More than a little miracle. A huge one."

"You can find them every time if you look.

Thanks for being mine,'' Lori said. His eyes held all the miracles she would need for a lifetime, and they promised his love for just as long. That was the best miracle of all.

* * * * *

Dear Reader,

Friedens, Missouri, is not a real place. At least, you won't find it on any map. I've gotten quite familiar with it in the course of the past six months, though. So familiar that I didn't want to leave it behind as I have most of my fictional places. Friedens (which is German for "peace," in honor of the German settlers like my ancestors who built most of the towns in eastern Missouri) is a combination of a dozen of my favorite real Missouri towns. They're those places that still have a county courthouse, a real town square and a solid brick-and-stone library.

The town square has turned into antique shops and craft stores and restaurants to keep the town café company. And I had Friedens reflect this. Maybe knowing so much about all those places made me reluctant to leave the town behind.

In any case, Steeple Hill has been kind enough to let me stay on in Friedens. Look for Carrie's story, and those of her two older sisters, all set in my favorite town.

I love hearing from readers, especially those who share my love of small towns that make the heartland of America what it is. You can contact me at: P.O. Box 514, St. Peters, Missouri 63376.

Yours in Christ,

Lynn